```
Fic      Giff, Patricia
Gif         Reilly
C. 1.       Have you seen
            Hyacinth Macaw?
```

DATE DUE

APR 30 '82	APR 6 '84	NOV 27 '85	JAN 9 '87
MAY 26 '82	APR 13 '84	JAN 10 '86	FEB 20 '87
Murphy	OCT 12 '84	JAN 17 '86	MAR 6 '97
OCT 15 '8	FEB 22 '85	JAN 31 '86	APR 10 '87
OCT 29 '82	APR 12 '85	MAR 7 '86	MAY 22 '87
JAN 21 '83	APR 26 '85	APR 4 '86	FEB 0 0
FEB 25 '83	MAY 10 '85	APR 11 '86	NOV 0 0
MAR 11 '83	MAY 17 '85	APR 25 '86	
MAY 26 '83	SEP 27 '85	MAY 2 '86	
OCT 21 '84	OCT 4 '85	MAY 23 '86	
NOV 11 '82	NOV 4 '85	OCT 30 '86	
JAN 27 '84	NOV 15 '85	DEC 19 '86	

HAVE YOU SEEN HYACINTH MACAW?

The adventures of Casey Valentine and her friends
by Patricia Reilly Giff,
illustrated by Leslie Morrill:

Fourth-Grade Celebrity
The Girl Who Knew It All
Left-Handed Shortstop

HAVE YOU SEEN HYACINTH MACAW?

PATRICIA REILLY GIFF

Illustrated by ANTHONY KRAMER

DELACORTE PRESS/NEW YORK

Published by
Delacorte Press
1 Dag Hammarskjold Plaza
New York, N.Y. 10017

Manufactured in the United States of America

First printing

LIBRARY OF CONGRESS CATALOGING IN PUBLICATION DATA

Giff, Patricia Reilly.
Have you seen Hyacinth Macaw?

SUMMARY: Abby and her friend Potsie work on several mysteries: a mysterious new neighbor, a missing person, a theft, and the unusual actions of Abby's brother.
[1. Mystery and detective stories. 2. City and town life—Fiction] I. Kramer, Anthony. II. Title.
PZ7.G3626Hav   [Fic]   80–68729

ISBN 0–440–03467–1
ISBN 0–440–03472–8 (lib. bdg.)

For the memory of
Jeanne Tiernan Millan
and for
Robert Cameron Millan
with love

DATE: Sunday, April 4. (No schl this wk. Sprng vac.)
TIME: 9:00 P.M.

Spent aftnoon looking for muggers.
No muggers.

How can practice to be detective when no mystery?
HAVE TO KEEP LOOKING.

M is for Marjorie.

CHAPTER 1

With her brother's binoculars slung around her neck, Abby Jones knelt on the chair next to her bedroom window. One story below, dozens of people rushed around in the rain.

She watched them, looking for someone to focus on. Someone who looked like a criminal. A kidnapper, maybe. Or a murderer.

"Looking for killers again?" a voice asked behind her.

Abby jumped. "Don't be silly."

Her brother, Dan, took a thick red pad out of his pocket and waved it at her, grinning.

"Hey!" She scrambled toward him. "That's my private property."

She tried to grab it, but even though Dan was only a

year older than she, he was much taller. He held it out of her reach. "I read the whole thing," he said, "but it's your own fault. You left it in my room."

"I did not," she said hotly. "I wasn't even in your room." Then she remembered the binoculars. Instinctively she covered them with her hands. She must have left the memo book on his dresser when she pulled the binoculars out of his drawer.

"Memo for Sunday," Dan said in a high screeching voice, pretending to imitate her. "Looked for muggers all afternoon. . . ." He broke off, spotting the binoculars. "Did you take those again?"

Abby pulled the binoculars over her head. "They're rotten anyway. All blurry. I can see just as well without them." She took a step back. "But you're not going to get them back, until I get my . . ."

"Notebook?" Dan finished for her, still waving it around.

"Not notebook. Memo book. All the cops in New York City have memos. They write down everything they do all day. It helps them out with clues and stuff. Garcia told me."

"Red memos?"

Abby shrugged. "They have black leather ones. But red is my trademark."

Dan wasn't listening. He tossed the memo book on her bed. "Where's my comb? I have to go to work in a little while."

"How should I know?"

"Because you're always borrowing it."

She shrugged. "It's on the dresser. Just because you've got a part-time job sweeping up bird goop in the pet shop twice a week, you think you're the king of the world." She narrowed her eyes, trying to picture what he'd look like with decent ears and a haircut. His ears stuck out terribly, and his brown hair flew around in a million directions.

She touched the top of her head gingerly. With her wiry hair and her two broken front teeth that made a small upside down V, she was no beauty, either.

She handed Dan the binoculars and, as he went back down the hall, slammed the door behind him as hard as she could. The whole apartment seemed to vibrate. Then she reached for a candy kiss on the table next to her bed, took off the silver wrapper, and popped it into her mouth.

She was really mad at herself for yelling at Dan. She licked her fingers. It was kind of lonesome now that her mother and father had gone to New Jersey to buy motors and parts for their used-car-lot business. She'd try to stay away from his things for a while. At least until her parents came home.

Suddenly, behind her, there was a crash.

She jumped. There must be new people in the empty apartment next door. She thought she had heard someone yesterday but Dan had said she was crazy.

She'd show him who was crazy. She stood up and tiptoed to the wall. Sometimes it wasn't so bad having this peanut of a room stuck between Dan's bedroom and apartment 2B next door.

She leaned against the wall, listening. She could hear a faint scrabbling sound and then a clunk. Something dropping.

Maybe it was a body.

She wished she could hear what was going on in there. She remembered reading somewhere that listening through a glass—

She raced down the hall to the kitchen. Mrs. Eggler, the neighbor who was staying with them while her parents were away, was sitting reading, her feet on a chair. She shoved her glasses up on her gray hair as Abby came into the kitchen. "Have any interesting dreams lately?" she asked.

Abby tried to think of something. Eggie was always asking about their dreams. She loved to try to figure out what they meant.

"I dreamed about the police department," Abby said hurriedly, fingers crossed behind her back. "I was helping them solve a big case."

"That means good luck." Mrs. Eggler tapped the book on her lap. "It says so right here in *Madame Zera's Dream Book*. And even if it didn't, I'm getting so good I can think of the answers myself."

"That's good." Abby opened the kitchen cabinet and took out a glass. "I'll just take this glass along to my bedroom."

"An empty glass?"

"I'll fill it with a little water."

Mrs. Eggler shook her head as Abby held the glass under the faucet and filled it halfway. "I'm going down to the store now, Abby," she said. "I'll be back in a little while."

Abby backed out of the kitchen. "I'll be in my bedroom." She rushed down the hall, stopping to dump the water into her mother's pink geranium; then, back in her room, she shut the door.

For a moment she stood there against the wall, turning the glass around. "Which end?" she muttered to herself.

"What?"

She spun around. It sounded as if a boy were standing directly behind her.

"Ssh," someone hissed.

"What?" he said again.

Abby opened her mouth to answer him.

"Will you be quiet?" someone said in a furious whisper.

Abby twisted her head around trying to hear better. The boy's mother? His father? She couldn't tell.

She grabbed the glass, put the bottom against the yellow flowered wallpaper, and leaned her ear against the other end. She listened carefully but all she could hear was an oceany sound that the empty glass made against her ear.

She turned the glass around so the rim was against the wall and put her ear to the bottom. There was a faint scrabbly noise. She listened to it for a moment, trying to figure out what it was.

Suddenly there was a scream. It was loud and high-pitched. It seemed to last for a long time. Abby jumped back from the wall. She felt a shiver start at her neck and ripple down the length of her back. The glass slipped out of her hand and bounced off the edge of her wastebasket onto the rug.

CHAPTER 2

Abby didn't bother to pick up the glass. She raced out of her bedroom and down the hall to Dan's room.

His door was locked. "Dan," she yelled, "let me in."

Her voice echoed back in the empty apartment. He must have left for work. She wondered why he had locked his door. She hadn't even known there was a key for his room.

She shivered again and went slowly back into her room and sat on the edge of her bed. She listened for several minutes but nothing more seemed to be happening in the next apartment. She reached for the memo book.

No pencil. She leaned over the side of the bed to look for one. She hung there resting her head on the floor, watching the dust balls moving gently under the bed.

Her mother would have a fit if she knew how Eggie kept house.

She sat up and rooted around in the table drawer until she found a pencil. She chewed on it a little to sharpen the point and smoothed the book with her hands. Outlined in green on the red cover were the words KEEP OUT NOSEY and underneath, in blue, ABBY M. JONES.

She was going to change her name as soon as possible, the minute she hit fifteen, sixteen at the latest. Abigail Jones was much too plain. In the meantime, whenever she wrote a memo, she slipped a new initial or name in to see how it looked.

She opened to a new page, thought for a moment, and began to write. As she scribbled down what had happened in the next apartment, she wondered if she had imagined the scream. Maybe it was just a new kid playing tricks on her.

She got off the bed and wandered over to the window. Downstairs there was a mess of traffic and umbrellas bobbing around.

A square of white tacked to the telephone pole on the corner caught her eye. She could just about see the words on the top. They said: HAVE YOU SEEN.

She squinted, wishing she had Dan's binoculars. Slowly she made out the words on the next line: HYA-CINTH MACAW?

There was smaller writing underneath, but even though she stared until she felt her eyes were crossing, she couldn't tell what the words said.

Then, from the corner of her eye, she spotted a girl rushing down the street. She held a red-and-white

polka dot umbrella over her head and wore a green T-shirt with purple flowers on it.

— The girl stopped to read the sign, then suddenly ripped the sign in a jagged line down the center. The torn ends were left, flapping in the wind. Swiftly she crossed the street, dodging between the cars, and walked to the middle of the block. When she reached the pet shop, she opened the door and poked her head in. Then, almost as if she could feel Abby watching her, she spun around and looked directly up at Abby's apartment house. She stood there for a few seconds, then turned and continued down the street.

Very peculiar, Abby thought when she was out of sight. Why would she tear that sign down?

— Then Abby saw two men coming down the street. One of them was Witkowski, and the other was Garcia.

She shoved her memo book into her pocket and went over to the closet for her rain gear. Two minutes later she was out of the apartment and down the stairs, still jamming her yellow rain hat on her head.

She caught up with the men as they turned into Coco's Diner on the corner.

The diner was noisy and crowded. She walked carefully around Witkowski and was lucky enough to get the last seat at the counter, right next to Garcia.

"Hey," she said. "How come you're working today?"

Garcia grinned. He had been her friend ever since second grade when he had visited her school and told them all about crime prevention.

She grinned back. No one would ever guess that Garcia was a detective. Under his open leather jacket, he was wearing an orange sweat shirt that said I'M A CRAZY GUY. It was ripped in about four places.

"Just because you're on spring vacation, do you think I should be, too? Besides, I have to check something out today." He looked toward the door. "Where's your friend Potsie today?"

"Shopping with her mother."

On the other side of Garcia, Witkowski leaned over toward her. He had a sharp-looking nose and crinkly orange hair. "Are you here again?" he asked, raising one of his pale eyebrows.

Abby ignored him and fiddled with a napkin.

"What do you want, Abby?" Garcia asked. "A hamburger? Soda?"

"Coffee," she said to the woman who was waiting to take their orders.

The woman raised her eyebrows.

"With lots of milk. Mostly milk," she said.

"Three coffees," Garcia said, "and a couple of hamburgers."

The woman turned her back on them to pour the coffee. Then she slammed the cups on the counter and shoved the milk pitcher toward Abby.

Abby poured in some milk and raised the coffee up to her mouth as carefully as she could. The last time she had been here with Garcia and Witkowski she had spilled an egg cream on the counter. And half of it had landed in Witkowski's lap.

"Check out what?" she asked Garcia again after she had swallowed a mouthful.

"A robbery," he answered.

"How much?"

"About two thousand dollars' worth."

Abby sighed and took another sip of her coffee. "You have all the luck. I can't wait till I'm a detective and get to investigate a whole bunch of cases."

On the other side of Garcia, Witkowski rattled his coffee cup. "Heaven help this city if you ever get into the Police Department."

Abby ignored him. "I have my memo book right here," she said. She reached into her pocket and pulled it out. "Do you want to give me some of the facts? I could kind of look around and let you know . . ."

She lowered her eyes to the memo book so she wouldn't have to look in the mirror behind the counter and see Witkowski laughing at her.

"It's a little complicated, Abby," Garcia said. He smothered his hamburger with pickle relish and took a huge bite.

Abby reached into her pocket and pulled out her pencil. "Just a rough idea," she said.

"The store owner figures one of the kids who work there may have done it. But we can't prove it yet."

Quickly Abby wrote ST OWNR THNKS WKR TK MONEY. "Do you think so, too?"

Garcia shrugged. "Hard to tell yet. I don't want to jump to any conclusions." He put the rest of the hamburger into his mouth.

"Where is the store?"

"On Washington Avenue," he said as soon as he could talk.

"Hey . . . where I live . . ." she began.

Witkowski stood up. "Come on, Garcia," he said. "Are you going to sit around here all day?"

"Witkowski's in a hurry," Garcia said. He slid off the stool and fished through his pockets for change.

She waved and watched as they walked toward the cashier. "Garcia," she called, suddenly remembering. "You forgot to tell me the name of the store."

Garcia turned and said something before he closed the door, but she couldn't hear him.

She shook her head in irritation. Washington Avenue ran along forever. Garcia always seemed to do that to her. He told her a bunch of facts but never got to the good stuff. She'd have to wait till the next time she saw him. But in the meantime, she thought as she finished her coffee, she'd keep a good watch on Washington Avenue.

DATE: Monday, April 5.
TIME: All different.

1. Horrble scrm next door.
    kid doing it?
    maybe a MURDER. (I hope.)
2. *****CRIME*****
    ST OWNR THINKS WKR TK MONEY.
    Wash. Ave.
3. Who is HYACINTH MACAW?
    Why did girl tear sgn?

CHAPTER 3

A watery sun shone into Abby's bedroom the next morning. She lay in bed for a while wondering about Garcia's robbery, then swung her legs over the side. There was a werewolf movie around the corner this week. If Dan would lend her a little money, she and Potsie could go to see it this afternoon.

She threw on her old pink robe and went down the hall to his room.

"Hey," she called into the open bedroom. "Are you awake?"

She waited a minute for him to answer, then poked her head around the door. He was probably in the kitchen having breakfast. She looked around trying to see what he had done with the binoculars, but they were nowhere in sight.

His room was so messy she wondered how he could

find anything. Shirts were draped over the dresser. Books and papers were scattered all over. Even the floor felt gritty.

His closet door was half open and a green blanket was thrown over something inside. It made a knobby-looking package that was as high as her waist.

She wondered what it was. She took a couple of steps into his room. Suddenly, behind her, something clamped down on her shoulder. Hard.

She jumped and shook Dan's hand off. "You big dope," she shouted. "You nearly scared me to death."

Dan threw himself on the bed laughing. "The big detective," he said. "Scared of her own shadow."

She felt like throwing something at him. Then she remembered the movie. "I was just looking for you," she said in her friendliest voice. "How about lending me some money."

He got up off the bed. For a minute he didn't answer her. "No," he muttered finally.

"You stingy thing. You have a job."

"I have to pay for a window I broke," he said. "Right away. Even the money from the job won't be enough. It's a good thing we have another way . . ."

"Whose window? What do you mean . . . we?" Abby broke in.

His mouth clamped shut in a tight line. When he looked like that she knew she'd never get another word out of him.

"Well," she said, sighing, "I guess it wasn't such a hot movie after all."

She turned and went back into the hall. "Hey," she said, leaning her head around the door. "Why did you lock your room yesterday? Where did you get a key?"

He hesitated. "If you're such a great detective," he said after a moment, "you should be able to figure it out."

"Well, I can't," she answered, "so tell me."

He laughed. "I'll give you a clue. Two clues. One, I've got a sister who keeps borrowing my stuff. Two, there were a bunch of keys in the kitchen drawer."

From the kitchen came the sound of Eggie's voice. "Breakfast, kids."

Abby could hear her rattling the pots around. Making oatmeal probably, the kind with lumps.

Abby followed Dan down the hall and sat down at the kitchen table. "Oatmeal?" she asked.

"How did you guess?" Eggie smiled, creasing her face into dozens of lines. She handed them both a bowl.

Abby took hers gingerly. "We had pancakes yesterday and eggs the day before. Figured today was oatmeal." It looked even worse than she had expected. She took a spoonful.

Mrs. Eggler stood there waiting. "Good?"

Abby opened the cabinet door. "I think it needs a few raisins." She sprinkled a bunch on top. "I have to hurry anyway. Can't take much time to eat. I promised I'd call for Potsie the first thing this morning." She swallowed another spoonful of her cereal.

Across from her, Dan's head was practically buried in his bowl. Just like a horse, she thought. He didn't even seem to realize the oatmeal was terrible. Thick and gluey.

Eggie handed Dan a piece of burned toast. "I dreamed of a horse last night," she said, shaking her head. "I haven't had time to look it up, but I think it means someone is going to run away."

Dan looked up, his brown eyes crinkling. "I hope it's Abby."

Abby stuck her tongue out at him.

"What did you kids dream about?" Eggie asked.

"I dreamed about some nutty girl pretending she was a detective," Dan said.

Eggie looked at him. "I can't figure that one out," she said. "I'll have to look in *Madame Zera's Dream Book*."

"Got to run," Dan said. "Great cereal."

"Where are you off to?" Eggie asked.

Dan hesitated. "Going down the avenue."

"How far?"

Dan shrugged. "I Street." He slid out of his chair. As he went around the table, he put his face up close to Abby's and yelled, "Stick 'em up."

She jumped and swatted at him with her hand.

He went down the hall laughing. "Some detective," he yelled back over his shoulder.

"You'd be surprised," she said, and turned back to Eggie. "Do you know a girl named Hyacinth?"

Eggie shook her head. "I know that if you dream of wildflowers it means you're going to have an adventure."

"Are you sure you haven't seen her?" Abby asked. "Think. Maybe at the store or something?"

Eggie shook her head. "No. Who is it?"

"I don't know. I saw it on a sign. Funny name, isn't it?"

"It's a flower. You know, those bluish, purplish things."

Abby nodded as she popped the last three raisins from her cereal into her mouth. She stood up thinking that the girl who had ripped the sign down had had those purplish flowers all over her T-shirt. She put her bowl, with a half inch of oatmeal stuck to the bottom, in the sink.

Back in her bedroom she rooted around in the closet for some jeans and a top.

Behind her something rattled. She twisted her head and listened.

For a moment all she could hear was the sound of traffic in the street outside. Then she heard it again. Crunching. Or crackling.

She knelt down to look under the bed. Her room was getting so dirty that things must be starting to grow under there. She hoped it wasn't mice. The last time Eggie had stayed with them, Abby had left a half-eaten banana in her wastebasket. By the time they had cleaned her room, the whole basket was alive with little flying gray things.

There was nothing under the bed except the same old dustballs . . . and the noise. "Sounds as if it's right on top of me," she said aloud. "Hey . . ." She raised her head quickly to look around the room and banged the back of her head against the footboard. "2B," she whispered, rubbing her head.

She crawled over to the wall and listened. Here the noise was louder. It seemed to be coming from directly behind the molding.

She tried to remember which of the rooms in the apartment was next to hers. The bedroom? The kitchen? She hadn't been in there for the last two families. It must have been at least three years since a girl had lived there.

She thought for a second and shrugged. There had to be a new boy next door. Maybe he had heard her open the door.

Briskly she knocked on the molding. "I know you're in there," she said, mouth against the wall. "You'd better just watch out."

"Dr-i-i-p," the voice whispered back.

Abby jumped. "You're going to find out who's the drip around here," she whispered. "Don't fool around with me."

She didn't wait for him to answer. Instead she slammed back into her closet and grabbed up a pair of jeans from the floor and an orange shirt off a hanger.

She shrugged into her shirt, listening to the soft chuckling that was coming from the next apartment. Then she shoved her memo book into her jeans, and closed the bedroom door behind her. Her best friend, Potsie, was waiting for her.

CHAPTER 4

Outside at the curb Abby picked up a dirty Popsicle stick and sent it on its way to the sewer. Then she watched a pale worm wiggling through a puddle.

Suddenly someone bumped into her and almost knocked her off her feet. Abby turned and saw Kiki Krumback, the super's daughter. Kiki was plump as a pillow and had long, flowing red hair.

She put her face up close to Abby's and stared at her with pale blue eyes that looked like marbles. "Sorry, I didn't look where I was going. Are you all right?"

Abby sighed. Kiki Krumback was the most absent-minded girl she knew. "It's all right," Abby said as Kiki wandered down the block mumbling something about looking for some butterflies to paint.

Abby started to cross the street then remembered the sign and went to take a look.

It was a soggy mess.

She smoothed the pieces against the telephone pole and read:

HAVE YOU S

INTH MACAW?

SUBSTANTIAL REW   00

Telephone 555-944

Call   or nigh

Heartbroken

She narrowed her eyes. Reward. Substantial reward. Wonder how much?

Part of the telephone number was missing, too. She looked around on the sidewalk. There was a small, sodden piece of paper plastered against the bottom of the pole. She peeled it off. There was an uneven letter A scrawled on the scrap of paper.

She tried to match it to the rest of the sign but couldn't decide where it belonged. Maybe it should read A SUBSTANTIAL REWARD, she thought at last.

Carefully she removed the two pieces of paper from the telephone pole. No sense in letting the whole world in on the reward. Some detective like Witkowski would be falling all over himself, dusting for fingerprints, having lineups and investigations, and she and Potsie, who deserved all the credit, would get zilch.

She pulled her memo book out of her pocket, folded the sign inside, then raced across the street to Potsie's. In the hallway she pressed Potsie's bell and two or three other buttons and waited for someone to buzz back so she could open the door. She couldn't understand why everyone was so slow. She was always in a hurry.

Finally someone buzzed. Abby banged open the door and ran up the stairs.

Potsie's mother stood in front of her apartment door fooling around with a screwdriver and the front doorbell. "Go ahead in, Abby," she mumbled around two screws she was holding in her teeth. "Potsie's finishing up the dishes."

Abby smiled at Mrs. Torres as she slid around her. Inside the phone was ringing. "Get that, will you, Abby," Potsie said. "I'm up to my ears in dishwater."

Abby picked up the phone and listened. "A magazine salesman," she told Potsie after a minute.

Potsie nodded. "Give him the business."

Abby sat up on the kitchen table. "I would truly love to take a subscription to your magazine, Mr. . . . . What did you say your name was? Connors? Yes indeed, Mr. Connors. However," she went on, "it is simply impossible. You see, my dear daughter Potsie has come down with a rare and deadly disease. And of course, my money is completely tied up. . . ."

From the sink Potsie giggled.

"Yes indeed, Mr. uhm . . . Connors," Abby continued, "I have simply flown her all over the world . . . took a canoe down the Amazon to see some famous doctor. . . . Hello? Mr. Connors?"

Abby held the phone away from her ear and made a face. "What do you know! He hung up."

"Terrific job," Potsie said. "Even better than usual. Wish I could do that."

"And I wish my name were Penelope Olivia Torres." Abby grinned. "Listen, Potsie. We can't go to the movies. I asked Dan for some money but he said he has to save up for a window he broke."

Potsie nodded. "One of the kids told me that Dan and a girl—I think her name was Priest or something like that—were pushing a hockey puck around the street. They zoomed it right into a stained-glass window sitting in front of Peter Tanner's craft store. Old Pete was mad as hops. He said the window cost him fifty dollars to make, and he's going to give them one week to pay for it. Otherwise he's going straight to the police and turn them both in."

"My mother will have a fit if she finds out," Abby said uneasily. "No wonder Dan didn't want to tell me about it. There's stuff going on all over the place. Garcia has a robbery right on Washington Avenue, and there's a new kid in the apartment next to me who's going to get his teeth knocked out, and . . ." She flipped open her memo and removed the pieces of the sign. "Still a little damp," she said as she spread them out on the counter, "but you can get the general idea. Some idiot girl tried to rip this sign off a telephone pole. Maybe she wants to solve the mystery herself."

She flicked the paper with her index finger. "Somebody's lost or kidnapped, or killed for all I know. I wonder if you get the reward if the person's dead. Discover the body . . ."

"What are you talking about?" Potsie asked, leaning over her shoulder. "Who's been killed? How? Strangled?" Potsie shivered.

"Don't jump overboard, Potsie. Maybe she isn't dead yet. It could be amnesia." She ran her hand over her forehead and closed her eyes. "I can't remember a thing," she said slowly, "but I seem to remember that my name is Hyacinth." Her eyes widened. "Hey. Eggie dreamed about somebody running away. Maybe it was Hyacinth. Maybe her parents are heartbroken."

She shook her head. "It's the first time Eggie's ever had any of this dream business right. I dreamed about a nurse last year and she said I was going to get some money. Probably be rich. I was so excited. . . ."

She smoothed out the pieces of the sign. "I haven't had more than twenty cents in my pocket at a time since then."

Potsie nodded slowly and reached into a kitchen drawer for a package of gum. "Last piece," she said. "Sorry." She unwrapped the paper. "I chewed it before breakfast. Just wrapped it up again." She popped it into her mouth and looked at the sign. "Wonder how much reward. Ten dollars?"

"Ten? Are you crazy? If your daughter had run away, would you give ten dollars? How about a thousand, or ten thousand? Much more like it."

Potsie blew a bubble. "You could be right."

"If we had the whole phone number," Abby said, "we could find out right now."

Potsie looked at the sign. "There are six numbers

here. There should be seven. It looks like the last one is missing."

Abby reached for her memo book. "You're right, Pots, old girl. So it shouldn't be so hard to figure out the right number. Hand me a pen, will you?"

She flipped to a new page and numbered from one to nine.

Potsie hopped up on the kitchen table and pushed the phone toward Abby. "Go to it."

Abby picked up the receiver. "I think I'll start with nine." She dialed 555-9449 and waited. "Nobody's home," she began, and broke off. "Hello? What do you mean, What time is it? Late. Time to get up. Listen, I'm a friend of Hyacinth's."

She listened for a minute, then shrugged and clunked the phone receiver down. "Wrong number." She put a check next to the number nine.

"You want to try the next one, Potsie? I don't want to hog this whole thing. Try eight."

Potsie squeezed her nose with two fingers and dialed.

"Hello?" she said in a loud nasal voice. "I want to talk to you about Hyacinth."

She covered the phone with her hand. "He said 'about what?' "

"What do you mean, about what?" Potsie continued. "How much is the reward?"

Potsie shook her head and hung up. "Here comes my mother," she said, motioning toward the front door. "We'd better get out of here. She said our bill last month was horrible."

Abby grabbed her arm. "What did he say?" she asked. "How much? Ten thou?"

Potsie jumped off the table. "It was a flower shop," she said. "He thought we wanted to buy some hyacinths."

"Potsie," said Mrs. Torres from the kitchen door. "Are you and Abby on that telephone again? Your father said he tried to call me last Saturday for one hour and the phone was busy, busy, busy."

"Let's get out of here," Potsie said. "I guess that's the end, end, end of the phone calls."

CHAPTER 5

They dashed out the door, hesitated at the elevator, then ran down the three flights of stairs without stopping and collapsed on the steps in front of Potsie's building.

Potsie eased her feet out of her wooden clogs. "Half the kids in the world are wearing these," she complained, "but they really squish my feet."

Abby leaned back against the stone steps. "That's why I don't wear mine." For a moment she watched the people passing by. Then she sat up straight. "Hey, Pots. There's a sign on the pole at the other end of the street."

Lazily Potsie sat up. "Do you want to take a look?"

Abby jumped off the steps. "I'll go."

A minute later she was back, the sign in her hand. "It's pretty mushy from the rain." She spread it out on her lap. "Nothing important anyway. A new antiques shop. Justine's Junktiques. It says she's having some kind of contest. All the way downtown on Washington Avenue somewhere."

Potsie leaned over her shoulder and traced the words with her fingers. "What does that say down there? No . . . something."

Abby held it up to the light. "It looks like CHILDREN. What a nerve. NO CHILDREN." She crumpled it into a ball. "Who wants to enter her old contest anyway?"

Abby stretched her legs out as far as she could so the people passing in front of her had to walk around her. A bald man nearly tripped, and muttered as he flung out his hand to catch his balance.

"Sorry," Abby said absently, and tucked her damp sneakers underneath her.

Behind the man a girl, head bent, walked by swiftly. She was wearing a green T-shirt with a big pink H on it.

"Hey." Abby grabbed Potsie's arm. "There's the girl who tore down the sign."

"Skinny-looking thing, isn't she?"

"Look, she has an H on her shirt," Abby said slowly. "And yesterday it was flowers. Hyacinths, I bet. It all fits. She's probably the runaway."

Abby stood up and jumped off the steps. "Let's follow her."

She started after the girl. Behind her, Potsie shoved her feet into her clogs and clattered down the street after them.

As the girl turned the corner, Abby stopped and looked back at Potsie. "What's the matter with you? Everybody can hear you."

Potsie waved her hand. "Go ahead," she said. "I'll catch up."

Impatiently Abby watched her step out of her clogs, peel off her plaid socks, and tuck them into the clogs.

"Good thing the bottoms of my feet are like leather," Potsie said as she caught up, carrying the clogs.

"Hurry," Abby said. "We're going to lose her. She's crossing the street and there are a bunch of people on that side." She stood on tiptoes. "I think she's going toward the subway. Come on."

Abby dashed across the street, ignoring the cars. Behind her Potsie hobbled along, and up ahead the girl in the green T-shirt marched into the subway entrance.

"I knew it," Abby moaned as she saw the bright T-shirt disappear down the steps. She put on a burst of speed and took the stairs two at a time as she fished through her pocket for money. "Three cents," she yelled back to Potsie. "How about you?"

"A nickel."

Abby smiled apologetically at the furious man in the token booth as she and Potsie ducked under the turnstile. "Pay you double next time," she shouted, afraid he'd come after them.

They rushed down the stairs and onto the downtown platform. Abby craned her neck trying to look around the crowd of people waiting for the train to come in. Finally she spotted the girl standing at the edge of the

35

platform. She motioned to Potsie and eased up behind the girl.

Up close, she could see that the girl was a year or two older than they were. A strand of black hair lay across her cheek.

Abby leaned forward to get a better look. The girl had a long pointy nose and a skinny little mouth. She swiveled around and stared at Abby, green eyes narrowed.

Quickly Abby jumped back and pretended to be reading an advertisement for Sure Thing spot cleaner. "Have you ever tried any of this stuff?" she asked Potsie as the girl continued to stare at her. "Terrific stuff. My mother swears by it."

Potsie looked at her as if she had gone crazy.

"Yes, sir," Abby repeated lamely. "Terrific stuff."

With a roar the train exploded into the station and screeched to a stop. The girl slid between the doors as they were still opening and beat an old man to the last empty seat by half an inch.

Potsie hesitated but Abby gave her a little push. They followed the rest of the crowd into the train, making sure that they stayed as far away from the girl as they could and still keep an eye on her.

She wasn't paying any attention to them anyway. She was looking up trying to read the old man's newspaper as he leaned on the strap in front of her.

"Ow. Watch out for my feet, will you," Potsie said. "They may be made of leather, but they're not iron."

"Did I step on you? Sorry." She looked down at Potsie's feet. They were filthy.

A woman standing next to them looked down, too. "Why don't you put your shoes on?" she asked in a shrill voice. "That's a good way to pick up a fungus or athlete's foot."

Abby winked at Potsie. "She has a dread skin disease anyway," Abby said to the woman. "It's called leatheritis. It causes your toes to drop off eventually." She smiled sweetly. "I'm afraid it's catching."

The woman moved away from them and so did one or two other people who were standing nearby. The old man looked over his shoulder and winked at them.

Abby nudged Potsie. "I forgot. We're supposed to be incognito," she whispered.

"What's that?"

"Invisible. Nobody's supposed to know we're here. Especially," she said, covering her mouth, "that girl who's staring at us again."

At that moment, the train stopped and the doors opened. The girl ducked around the man with the newspaper and slid out the door.

Abby dove after her. A second later she turned to look for Potsie. She was waving frantically from inside the train as it pulled away from the station. Abby stood there shaking her head, then she raced up the stairs after the girl.

As Abby watched from the subway entrance, the girl stopped at a newsstand and bought a Hershey bar, then crossed the street and looked in a bakery window.

Abby left the subway entrance and sauntered over to the newsstand. She paged through a movie magazine until the girl continued down the street. As the girl turned the corner, Abby crossed the street and raced after her.

But it was too late. By the time Abby reached the corner, the girl was gone. Abby wanted to scream. There were about four apartment houses on each side of the street and the girl could have gone into any one of them.

Abby looked around trying to decide what to do. Finally she climbed the three steps of the first building and tiptoed into the vestibule. She stamped over to the mailboxes and studied the names. "About a thousand," she said to herself. "The girl could be anyone."

She ran her finger along the metal boxes. Some of the names were typed neatly, others had been written in pen and were faded or runny, and some had no names at all. Should she ring a bell and look around upstairs? Or should she give up and go home?

She looked up at the street sign. Washington and I. She lived uptown, two blocks past A, half the alphabet away. But it was only one stop on the subway. Good thing. Otherwise she'd have ended up on the other side of the city instead of ten or twelve streets from home.

And what about Potsie? she though irritably. That dummy was probably riding around taking a tour of the city. Or lost.

What a pair of detectives they were.

A huge man with stringy black hair stamped out of the lobby into the vestibule. He was carrying a mop and a bucket smelling of ammonia water. He set the bucket down. "What do you want?" he asked.

"I'm uhm . . . waiting for my cousin," Abby said. "She went upstairs for something."

"I didn't see any girl come in here," the man said.

"Didn't you see a girl in a T-shirt? Kind of ugly?"

"What's her name?"

"I don't know."

"I thought she was your cousin."

Abby jumped. "Oh, yes. Her name is . . . Clarabelle." She nodded. "Yes, Clarabelle Tykofski."

The man shoved his mop into the pail. "What do you think I am? Some kind of idiot? Clarabelle. Why don't you get out here, kid. Disappear."

"I must have the wrong building," Abby said, edging toward the door. "I think I'm supposed to wait for her across the street."

She walked out of the vestibule and went down the steps, watching the man over her shoulder as he mumbled, "Clarabelle."

Outside she hesitated. Finally she shrugged and went back down the street. If the girl was a runaway, maybe she was hiding out in this neighborhood. But what had she been doing uptown?

Twenty minutes later she was home. She stretched out on the stone steps in front of Potsie's apartment house and put her face up to catch the sun. She wondered what method Garcia would use to find out about a girl he was following.

She opened her eyes as she heard Potsie clatter down the street.

"Whew," Potsie said, stepping out of her clogs and collapsing on the step next to her. "Have I been all over this city! I was really scared. By the time I got off I was miles crosstown. Then I got mixed up coming back . . . lost my socks . . ." She broke off. "What happened?"

Abby shrugged. "Lost her," she said, a little embarrassed.

Potsie bent over and lifted one foot with both hands. "I think I've got a splinter." She put her foot down. "That girl is in this thing pretty deep. She's probably the murderer."

Abby laughed. "We haven't even found a body."

"She probably got rid of it . . . dumped . . ."

Abby sat up straight. "That's Hyacinth Macaw, all right. And she doesn't want anyone to find her. That's why she came uptown. She's ripping signs off the telephone poles."

Potsie rubbed her big toe. "She's probably going all over the city. If she gets rid of the signs, no one will have any clues."

Abby grinned. "Good thing she left part of that sign on the pole. If it takes the whole spring vacation, we'll find her again."

"And collect the reward," Potsie said, nodding.

Across the street a window on the second floor opened. Mrs. Eggler stuck her head out. "Abby," she screeched. "Get yourself home. Your mother's on the phone. She wants to say hello to you."

FROM THE MEMO BOOK OF
ABIGAIL ANNA ALEXANDRIA JONES

DATE: Tuesday, April 6.
TIME: 8:30 P.M. (around)

1. Look for some keys:
    a. So can get in Dan's rm. (Can borrow stuff like binocs.)
    b. Can lock my rm too.
2. *****GARCIA'S CASE*****
        no news.
3. HYACINTH:
        runaway!!!!!
        looks like: skinny, ugly, pointy nse.
4. Mom and Dad telephone call.
    a. Mom says what's with Dan. He sounds different....worried about something??? Said to watch out for.
    b. Didn't want to tell Mom he has to pay for window he brke. Also locking doors. Will watch out.

CHAPTER 6

"Nice to get up in the morning and not have to rush off to school," Abby told Potsie. They were leaning against the bus-stop sign in front of her apartment house. Plastered across the top of the sign was a sticker. It said: JUSTINE'S STORE GIVES YOU MORE.

Potsie peeled it off and twirled around the pole. "What do you want to do today?"

Abby narrowed her eyes. "Too bad we had to lose that girl. We could have had a great time following her around all day."

"Don't worry," Potsie said. "Next time she comes around, we'll be waiting. . . ." She broke off. "Hey, there's your brother."

Abby watched as Dan waited for the light, then crossed the street toward them. He was holding a bulky brown package under his arm.

He didn't see them until he was practically on top of them.

"What have you got there?" Abby said.

Dan jumped. "Why are you hanging around here?"

"Where do you expect me to hang?" Abby asked. "I'm right in front of my own apartment." She narrowed her eyes and stared at the package. "What's that?"

"What?"

"You know very well what," she said, sidling up to him. She cocked her head to one side to see the writing that was scrawled over one side of the package.

"You're always snooping into everything," Dan said. He covered the writing with one hand and skirted around them.

They stared after him as he went up the steps to the apartment house. "What's the matter with him?" Potsie asked.

Abby opened her mouth to answer, then she shrugged and looked away. Potsie hadn't seen the writing on the package, but she had. The initials H.M. were scrawled across the brown paper wrapping. And below them: I STREET.

She wondered what Dan was up to. He was in trouble over that broken window. Then he began locking his room. Now he's always snapping at her for snooping.

She straightened her shoulders. The heck with him. Let him have his secrets. H.M. could mean anything.

"Hey," Potsie said, shaking her arm. "Pay attention.

You've been staring into space for the last three minutes."

"Sorry," Abby said, and shook herself. Potsie was looking at her strangely.

"I started to tell you yesterday," Abby began quickly. She didn't want to think about Dan anymore. "Some bratty kid's just moved into 2B. He was laughing and carrying on in there Saturday."

Potsie shaded her eyes and looked up at Abby's building. "Funny we didn't see them move in," she said. "Too bad the shades are down."

Abby looked up. "They must have come when we were out somewhere. Let's go over to see Mrs. Krumback. Find out about them."

Mrs. Krumback, the super, was in the front hall, sweeping. She was fat like Kiki and had the same color hair. But, as usual, her reddish hair was rolled in little pink rubber rollers. "What do you kids want?"

"2B," Abby said. "Who moved in?"

"Nobody." Mrs. Krumback shook her head. "Not until next month."

"Come on," Abby said. "You know somebody's in there."

Mrs. Krumback started to sweep again. "Will you get out of here?" she said irritably. "The two of you do nothing but run back and forth all day tracking in dirt and making a mess. I'll be glad when school starts again."

"But I know . . ." Abby began.

"Did you hear me?"

"Come on, Potsie," Abby said. "Everybody's in a rotten mood. Let's go up to my room."

Upstairs they saw Mrs. Eggler sitting in the living room, feet up, reading one of Abby's Nancy Drew books.

"Terrific mystery," Eggie said. "I can't guess the ending."

Potsie leaned over her shoulder. "Easy. Nancy finds the will and the neighbors get the money and . . ."

Mrs. Eggler looked up grimly. "Thank you very much, Potsie. Now I don't even have to finish the book."

"Ooh," Potsie said, clapping her hands over her mouth. "I'm sorry."

"It's all right," Mrs. Eggler said. "I guess I'll finish it anyway." She looked up at Potsie. "Had any good dreams lately?"

Potsie screwed up her face, trying to think. "I know," she said finally. "I was at the dentist, having X rays."

"That means you're involved in a mystery." She nodded her head deliberately. "No doubt about it," she said, looking back at her book. "Surrounded by mystery." Her voice trailed off as she turned the page and began to read again.

Abby raised her eyebrows and motioned to Potsie. "Come on," she mouthed.

She led the way down the hall, glancing at Dan's door as they passed. She wondered if he had locked it again.

In her room, she told Potsie, "Don't mind the junk all

over the place. I'm not going to do much cleaning until the day before my mother gets home."

She bounced herself down on the bed. "Now, listen," she said. "We'll probably hear the boy in there any minute."

They sat there for what seemed to be a very long time. Finally Abby jumped off the bed. "We could probably sit around here all day, and who knows, they may be out to the store or something."

She walked over to the wall and leaned her ear against it. "We could go up to the roof and climb down the fire escape. There might be a window open or maybe the shade isn't pulled down all the way. We might get a peek inside."

Potsie squinched her eyes together. "Too high up for me."

"What's five floors?" Abby said. She opened her bedroom door. "Come on."

"Wait a minute, Abby," Potsie said, sliding off the bed. "Suppose they're home. Maybe they're in the kitchen, or sleeping, or . . ."

Abby stood there thinking. "You're right, Pots. I'll check first." She marched over to her night table and picked up the glass. "Super detector thing," she told Potsie. "Magnifies the sound."

She leaned against the wall and knocked on it briskly. "Hey, drip," she said. "Wake up in there." She put the glass on the wall and rested her ear on it. "Answer me."

"Nobody," she said after a minute.

"Are you sure?"

"Positive."

They tiptoed past Mrs. Eggler in the living room, let themselves out the door, and skipped down the hall to the elevator.

Abby leaned on the button. "Why is it," she said, "that the elevator is always in the basement when I want it up here?" She bent down to tie her sneaker laces. "Good thing I wore these; traction is better."

Potsie shivered. "Do you really think we should . . ."

"Of course."

"If Mrs. Krumback catches us, we'll . . ."

Abby shrugged. "Here comes the elevator, Potsie. Don't be such a chicken." They stepped in as the door opened.

A moment later, the elevator creaked to a stop on the top floor.

"Come on, Potsie," she said. "Let's see if we make good acrobats."

CHAPTER 7

"So far, so good," Abby said after they had climbed the iron stairs and pushed open the heavy doors that led to the roof. "We just have to figure out which fire escape belongs to 2B. Then we can zip right down to the second floor."

She trotted across the roof, and, on tiptoes, leaned over the wall that ran along the edge. "Come on over here. Wait till you see how little everything looks from up here."

She put her leg over the wall and rested her foot on the top rung of the ladder. Suddenly the wind felt stronger, and she began to wonder if she was really going to be able to climb down three floors. Her hands clenched the grainy surface until the little lines in her knuckles turned red. Carefully she swung her other leg over.

She was facing the television antenna on the roof across the way and could see the telephone wires that crisscrossed the street. She tried not to look down, but she couldn't help taking a quick peek at the traffic below.

It made her dizzy.

"Hurry up, Potsie," she said, eyes closed.

Cautiously Potsie stuck her head over the edge of the wall. "I don't think . . ." she began, and stopped. "Hey, Abby, watch out. Mrs. Krumback is right underneath sweeping. If she looks up, you're going to get caught."

Abby clenched her teeth and took a step down. If it weren't for that bratty kid in 2B, she'd forget about . . .

"I'm going downstairs in the elevator, Abby," Potsie said. "I'll keep her busy."

"Hey, Potsie, don't leave me . . ." Abby began, but Potsie had already dashed across the roof and was tugging at the heavy doors that led downstairs.

"Well, Abby," she told herself, "it's up to you now. You can climb back on the roof and be a scaredy cat, like Potsie, or forge ahead to 2B like a regular Nancy Drew."

Eyes shut tight, she inched her way downward. After a few minutes, she began to enjoy herself. Standing on the fourth-floor fire escape, she opened her eyes and glanced down at Mrs. Krumback. She was listening to Potsie, who was talking a mile a minute and waving her arms around like a roller coaster. Then Dan hurried by, head down. Where was he going now? He looked like a crook leaving the scene of a crime.

Abby put her foot on the next rung. When she reached the third-floor landing, she stopped to rest. Next to her, a gray cat dozed in a window. Abby peered inside. There was Kiki Krumback, the super's daughter.

Kiki's red hair was piled up on top of her head and she was stuffed into a black-and-white striped robe. She was painting a picture while she watched a quiz show on television.

Abby scrunched over to see the picture. It looked like a fat bird, maybe a blue jay, sitting on a dead tree. Or was it a fence? She leaned closer. On the other side of the window the cat arched its back and hissed.

"What's the matter, Pussums," Kiki asked in a baby voice. "Some buggy out there bothering you?"

Quickly Abby ducked below the window. Head down, she crawled to the ladder, reached for the next rung, and started for the second floor.

At last she reached the fire escape outside 2B. Below her, Potsie was still talking to Mrs. Krumback.

Abby looked at the two windows on the second-floor landing. Both of them belonged to 2B. The shades were drawn down to the sill. She still couldn't see inside.

As quietly as she could, she tried to raise one of the windows. It didn't budge. She tried the other. It opened easily.

Abby glanced down to be sure that no one was watching. Good old Potsie. She must have dropped something, because Mrs. Krumback was looking down all over the sidewalk.

Abby swung a leg over the window ledge, ducked her head to avoid the window, and pulled herself in.

She blinked a couple of times to get her eyes used to the darkness; then she jumped off the sill and banged her hip on something. The stove. She was in the kitchen.

Cautiously she looked around. The kitchen seemed bare, empty, as if no one lived there. She opened the refrigerator. The light didn't click on and there was nothing inside. But on the kitchen table was a bowl half full of some kind of mush and, next to it, half an egg-shell.

She tiptoed out of the kitchen and went into the hall. There was no rug on the floor and in the living room she could see that there was no furniture. She stood there hesitating, trying to get her bearings. Which room in this apartment was next to her bedroom?

Near her were two closed doors. She opened the first one a crack. Just an empty closet with a few old rusty coat hangers on the rod.

The other door must lead to the bedroom. Abby turned the knob carefully and gently pushed the door. As it swung open, a loud cry came from inside. It was too dark to see anything.

Abby jumped back. She could hear her heart thumping. The boy must have been in there all morning, sleeping.

"Dr-r-i-p," whispered the voice. Something in the room toppled over.

Suddenly Abby felt that the cry and the harsh whisper she had heard had not been made by an ordinary boy. And whatever was in the room was moving toward her.

She looked down the hall at the door, but it was too late to run out. She yanked the closet door open, ducked inside, and closed the door behind her.

CHAPTER 8

It seemed like an hour, but it was probably only a few minutes that Abby sat scrunched in the corner of the closet waiting for whoever was in the bedroom to come after her.

In the background, she could hear pounding. It seemed to keep time with the sound of her heartbeats. Finally she realized it might be Potsie at the door of the apartment, banging to be let in. She listened, trying to decide what to do.

Barely making a sound, she inched open the closet door and peered out.

Nobody was there.

She measured the distance to the front door with her eyes, then threw open the closet door. She heard a noise behind her, but didn't even turn around to look. She raced down the hall, yanked open the door, and flew out of the apartment into the corridor.

She ran right into Potsie.

"Oof," gasped Potsie. As soon as she had caught her breath, she held up a pink matchbook. "Look what I've got."

"Quick," Abby said. "Shut the door."

Potsie stuck the matchbook between the door and the jamb, and pushed the door shut. "You think you're the only detective around here," she said, grinning. "But I read about this. It'll keep the door from locking, and we can get in whenever we want."

"Somebody's in there."

"The boy?"

"I don't think so. I think . . . something . . . horrible." She glanced nervously at the door. "I'll tell you one thing. I'm not going back in there to find out."

Potsie's eyes widened. "You could have been . . ."

"Killed." Abby shivered. "Or worse."

"I can't think of anything worse."

Abby nodded grimly. "Neither can I. Let's not even wait for the elevator. The stairs are just as fast."

She pushed open the stairway door and started down the steps ahead of Potsie. Above them something crashed. A cat yowled and feet pounded down the stairs.

Abby and Potsie jumped back against the wall. A large gray cat dashed past them. "Pussums," Abby said.

Right in back of the cat pounded Kiki Krumback, her red hair streaming out in back of her, and huge gold hoops bouncing against her plump neck.

"Out of the way," she yelled.

"What's going on?" Abby called.

But by this time Kiki and the cat were on the stairway below them. Abby leaned over the banister. She caught a glimpse of the cat's tail as it rounded the landing and streaked out the open vestibule door into the street.

"The cat won," she told Potsie. She marched down the rest of the steps and navigated around Kiki, who was leaning against the open doorway, panting.

"I forgot to close the door," she said, "and Pussums slipped out." She moved a curl higher on her head. "I'd like to paint his portrait, but he just doesn't want to sit still." She shook her head and went outside.

"She's as crazy as her name," Potsie said, "but dumb. D-U-M. And absentminded, too. Someone in school told me the other day that she sat on her last painting before it was dry."

Abby laughed. She watched Kiki squeeze herself between the bumpers of two cars and jaywalk across Washington Avenue. "What do you want to do now?" she asked Potsie.

"Something far away from apartment 2B," Potsie said.

Abby nodded uneasily. "I don't even want to think about what's in that apartment. Maybe we should work on the Hyacinth Macaw mystery instead. We could make some phone calls. . . ."

"I don't have a cent," Potsie said, slapping at her jeans pockets.

"I do. Eggie gave me some money for lending her my

fake diamond ring last night. She said she had taken a nap and dreamed that she was going to see some old friends and she wanted to look her best. We can go over to Coco's Diner. Call from there."

Together they crossed Washington Avenue. Kiki was crouched down on her hands and knees at the curb looking under a maroon station wagon. "Here, kitty, kitty, kitty," she was calling in a husky voice.

They skirted around her and turned the corner. Abby took a deep breath as they passed Angelo's Pizzeria. "Smell that pizza."

Potsie stopped and looked in the door. "I wish we had money for a slice."

"Just wait till we find Hyacinth Macaw, Potsie, and get that reward. We'll have pizza every day. Even for breakfast."

In Coco's, Abby grabbed a couple of pale-green mints from the dish at the cash register and headed for the telephone booth in the back. She pretended she didn't notice the woman behind the counter glaring at them.

She and Potsie squeezed into the booth together. Reaching into her pocket, she dug out some coins and laid them in a row on the shelf under the telephone.

"Do you remember the numbers we called yesterday?" Abby wiggled around to dig into her other pocket. "I wrote everything down in my memo book."

She slapped at her jeans. "It's not here."

"Did you lose . . ."

"Maybe I left it in my bedroom." She tried to remember. "I was sure I had it."

"Never mind," Potsie said. "I'm pretty sure I know the numbers anyway. I think we called 555-9449 and 555-9448. We're ready for seven."

"I guess you're right." Abby dropped some money into the slot and dialed. "Hello," she said. "I'm calling about Hyacinth Macaw. No. *Hyacinth.*" She shook her head impatiently. "*Hy-a-cinth.*"

"Hard of hearing," she explained to Potsie a moment later as she hung up. "Said she never heard of Hyacinth MacCann."

"Try another one," Potsie said.

Abby hesitated. "This isn't working out very well. All my money is going. Potsie," she said slowly. "Let's call the station house and find out if Garcia is working this afternoon. We can go over there and get some professional tips. We can certainly use a few."

CHAPTER 9

Abby stuffed her hanky over her nose and mouth and dialed.

She waited until someone answered: "Sixty-fifth Precinct. Sergeant Ruggerio speaking."

"Sergeant," she said gruffly, "is Detective Garcia working today?"

"Who's calling, please?"

"I can't reveal that information," Abby said, "however, it is urgent that . . ."

"But who . . ."

"Right now," Abby continued firmly, "I am incognito. That means I can't reveal my name to anyone."

"I know what incognito means."

"I'm glad to hear that, Sergeant," she said in her deepest voice. "Will you please tell me if Detective Garcia is working?"

"Yes, he is. Just a min . . ."

Abby hung up gently. "He's there. Let's go."

At the counter, she stopped for another handful of green mints and a couple of toothpicks.

"Why don't you take all of them?" the woman said, and slammed down someone's coffee. "These kids are always in here, buying nothing, taking everything. . . ."

Abby ducked out the door. She handed Potsie a toothpick. "I don't know what she's so annoyed about. I didn't even use the bathroom this time."

She and Potsie dodged through the traffic on Washington Avenue, sped down A Street, and arrived, breathless, at Adams Street.

The station house on the corner was an old red brick building with columns in the front. It looked like a fortress. Four or five policemen, off duty, stood talking on the steps, and a police car, turret light revolving, was parked in front.

With Potsie right behind, Abby circled the station house. In the back there was a weedy patch of grass and some old tires and boxes that looked as if they had been there forever. Abby climbed on a box, moved over to make room for Potsie, and peered in the window.

The greenish room inside had five desks in a row and a big gray file cabinet.

Abby spotted the back of Garcia's dark curly head and rapped against the dusty window. Witkowski was at the next desk.

Garcia scraped back his chair and walked over to them. He pushed his nose against the pane and made a

horrible face. Then he shoved up the window. "Hi, kids," he said. "Solve any crimes lately?"

"Just what I wanted to talk to you about," Abby said. Witkowski snorted.

"Was that you on the phone? Why didn't you talk to me?" Garcia asked.

"I was in a hurry," Abby answered. "Besides, I thought you might tell us you were too busy to talk."

Garcia laughed. "I'm never that busy."

"I want to ask you," Abby said, "have you got any tips about being a detective. You know, following . . . I mean tailing suspects."

Garcia sat on the windowsill. "Who's the poor victim you're after?"

Abby waved her hand in the air. "Just a hypothetical question," she said. "Nobody in particular, I guess."

"I'll bet," Witkowski said from his desk.

"Well," said Garcia, "you have to stay far enough behind so the suspect doesn't spot you. Wear inconspicuous clothing. Don't draw attention to yourself."

Abby looked hard at Potsie, thinking about her clogs.

"Anything else?" Potsie asked quickly. She drew her feet underneath her.

Garcia stopped to think. "Don't make eye contact with the person you're following."

"Eye contact?" Abby repeated.

"Something in your eyes will give you away."

"And," said Witkowski, "the person you're following will remember you the next time he sees you."

Abby looked at Witkowski with surprise. Then she

smiled at him slightly. One of these days he might even get to be friendly, she thought.

As soon as he saw her smiling, Witkowski frowned and began to type rapidly with the first two fingers of each hand.

Abby turned back to Garcia. "Suppose you knew the suspect was hiding out in an apartment house, but you didn't know which one. What would you do to find her?"

Potsie nudged her.

"Or him," Abby added quickly.

"I knew she had somebody in mind," Witkowski said.

Garcia laughed. "I hope you're not thinking of searching anyone's apartment, Abby," he said, suddenly serious. "People have rights. And if you go into someone's apartment intending to search it, you're committing a burglary."

Abby opened her mouth to explain that that wasn't what she meant. She wanted to find out what apartment Hyacinth lived in.

Quickly she shut her mouth again. It might be smarter if she and Potsie kept the details of the case to themselves for a while.

In back of them came the sound of the church bell on the corner. It chimed four times.

"Yikes," Potsie said, "I just remembered. I'm supposed to be home to go to my grandmother's at four." She slid off the box and raced out of the yard. "See you tomorrow," her voice floated back.

"How is your two-thousand-dollar case coming along?" Abby asked.

Garcia shook his head. "Not too good."

"Have you got any clues?"

"It was probably a kid," Witkowski said. "We'll get him." He smirked. "Or her. And that reminds me," he told Garcia, "I've got to call the store owner." He frowned at Abby. "But not in front of a civilian."

Abby shrugged. She could take a hint. Police work was confidential. "I think it's time for me to get home now. I promised Eggie I'd help her stuff cabbages for supper."

"Sounds good. Listen, Abby. If you want to talk some more, you can always give me a call." Garcia winked at her and leaned on the window to close it.

"Wow," he said when the window didn't budge. "This is really stuck. I'll have to get a hammer or something." He wandered over to his desk.

Slowly Abby climbed off the box. In back of her she could hear Witkowski dialing a number. She stood absolutely still but Witkowski was speaking so softly she was able to hear only two words. One of them was Washington and the other was pet.

Slowly she walked through the weed-covered yard, turning the words over in her mind. Washington for Washington Avenue, of course. But why pet? Pet store? On Washington Avenue? Could it be that someone had stolen two thousand dollars from the pet store?

She thought of Dan. Impossible. Not him. But suddenly she felt cold all over. She crossed the street and headed for home.

*****EMERGENCY MEMO*****
(on scrap paper—have to lk around for memo b.)
GAIL REBECCA JONES

DATE: Wednesday, April 7.
TIME: 4:30 P.M.

1. Skillions of stores on Wash. Ave. Witkowski could be calling anyone. NO. I am sure it's pet shop.
2. Dan works in pt s.
3. Owner says wker did it.
4. Dan?
5. Cldn't be.....****BUT***
    Mom said Dan acting fnny. (Gone crazy?)
    Locking door all the time.
6. And what about Hyacinth Macaw? Runaway? Dan mixed up with?
    a. She looked in pet store on Monday.
    b. Looking for Dan?
    c. She lives on I Street.
    d. Dan went to I Street.
    e. He stole $2000 to help her get away? Maybe to Florida? Africa?
    f. Dan going to run away too?
7. GOT TO FIND OUT WHAT'S GOING ON. GET KEYS. SEARCH ROOM.

CHAPTER 10

Abby folded the scrap paper and put it under her pillow. She could hear Eggie talking to Dan. She shook her head and went down the hall to the kitchen.

Eggie was pulling bowls out of the cabinet. "Almost time to stuff the cabbages," she said, looking at Abby. "What's the matter?"

Abby shook her head. "Nothing."

Dan was sitting at the table munching on a bunch of potato chips. His mouth and chin were all greasy.

Abby swallowed hard and went over to the junk drawer.

"What are you looking for?" Eggie asked.

"Nothing much." She plunged her hands into a tangle of tools and papers. "This drawer is really a mess. Someone should clean it out."

Behind her, Dan hooted. "How about you?"

She ignored him and sifted through the clutter wondering if he had taken all the keys in the house. There had always been loose keys floating around and maybe another one of them would fit his door. She had to get into his room. She'd start by looking at that package.

Finally she banged the drawer shut and sat down at the table across from him.

He slid the potato-chips bag over toward her. "Have a few."

She reached into the bag and took a handful.

"A few," he said, "doesn't mean the whole thing."

She looked at him wondering how he could look so innocent. She tossed the bag back at him, suddenly angry. What trouble he was causing her. Her whole spring vacation was going to be ruined worrying about him.

Suddenly she noticed his scuffed brown wallet on the edge of the table. She tried not to stare at it. Maybe he kept the key to his room in his wallet. If she could just get her hands on it for a few minutes, she could grab the key out.

She looked around trying to think of something to do. Then she stood up and went over to the sink. Eggie had bowls all over the place. Casually Abby picked up a large yellow one and brought it over to the table.

"What are you doing with that?" Eggie asked.

"Just getting set up," she said quickly. "More room to stir things over here."

"Set them up someplace else," Dan said as she rested the bowl on top of the wallet.

"All right," she said. She slid the bowl partway off the table with the wallet underneath. Garcia couldn't have done better, she thought, as she searched for the wallet with her fingertips.

The bowl slipped through her hands and smashed on the floor.

Dan bent over and picked his wallet up. "Watch out for my stuff, will you," he said.

She got the broom and swept up the pieces, watching him out of the corner of her eye. He gave the wallet a swipe with his hand, then pushed it into his back pocket.

"Where's that recipe for the cabbage?" Eggie asked.

Abby looked up. "Did you look in the . . ."

"Looked everywhere. How about your memo book?"

Abby shook her head. "No," she began, and hesitated. She pictured herself cleaning up the last time she and Eggie had made stuffed cabbages. Bowls all over the kitchen. Bits of rice and meat and eggs smeared on the counter.

She had picked up the recipe so it wouldn't be ruined. And she had tucked it . . .

"You're right, Eggie," she said. "Absolutely right. I was looking for that a minute ago." She looked around. "I thought it was in here," she shrugged. "I'll look in my bedroom again."

She spent ten minutes in her room pulling her clothes out of her dresser drawers, throwing stuff out of her closet. Then she wandered around the rest of the apartment, looking.

But the memo book was gone.

She went back into the kitchen and looked at Dan accusingly. "Did you take my memo book?"

"The one that tells all about looking for muggers?"

She looked at him angrily. "Shut up about that, will you? Can't a person do anything around here without your getting into it?"

Dan shrugged. "You're the one who gets into everyone else's business."

"Where's my memo?"

"I haven't seen it."

"You'd better look in your room," she yelled.

"Don't fight," Eggie cut in. "Please."

"He's got my memo book," she said, near tears.

"I don't," he said. "Word of honor."

"If we're going to stuff cabbages," Eggie said, "now's the time. Before it gets to be breakfast instead of supper."

Abby looked at her and tried to smile. Eggie really hated to see them fight. Then she frowned. It was a good thing Eggie didn't know some of the things that were going on.

"We can do it without the recipe," Eggie was saying. "Throw something together. It will probably taste even better than . . ."

Behind them, the phone rang.

"I'll get it," Abby said. "It's probably Potsie." She dashed down the hall into the living room and picked up the phone.

"Pots?"

"Is Daniel there?" a girl asked in a low voice.

"Daniel?" Abby repeated. "Daniel?" She began to

laugh. She couldn't remember anyone who ever called him Daniel. She looked back toward the kitchen, hoping he hadn't heard her. "Who is this?" she asked, putting her mouth close to the receiver.

At that moment, Dan came racing down the hall. "That's for me. Not you," he yelled. "It's none of your business what they want." In his hurry he tripped over the footstool and his wallet flipped out of his pocket.

As he stumbled to his feet, Abby grinned and handed him the phone. "Here, Daniel," she said.

He took the phone and turned his back toward her. She walked past him nonchalantly and gave the wallet a quick kick with the toe of her sneaker. It slid under the couch.

She continued down the hall walking as softly as she could so she could hear what he had to say.

"Tomorrow night?" he whispered. "Are you sure it's tomorrow? Don't worry. I'll be ready."

On Scrap Paper (Will Copy When Get M. BK. BACK)
FROM THE MEMO BOOK OF
ABBY M. WORTHINGTON-JONES

DATE: Wednesday, April 7.
TIME: 11:00 P.M.

******WHAT'S DOING TOMORROW NIGHT******

1. Tell Potsie about Dan. Potsie best friend. Have to trust.
2. Chk out wallet when he leaves apt. See if key inside. (Not stealing. His own fault for dropping. Besides...am trying to save him.)
3. Who called him? Hyacinth?
4. Where did memo book go?

List places I was today.		
Lost in street?	NO.	
Potsie's apartment?	NO.	
Stolen?	Maybe?	
Apartment 2B.	No.	YES.

TROUBLE. HAVE TO GET BACK.

M is for Mary.

CHAPTER 11

Abby stuck her head out of the bedroom door. "Eggie," she yelled. "Can I ask Potsie to stay overnight?"

"It's eleven o'clock," Eggie's voice floated back.

"Let me call, please," Abby begged. "Just to see. Maybe . . ."

There was no answer from the kitchen.

"Eggie? Are you there? Can I?"

"Ask her to come for supper tomorrow night instead."

"I will. Ask her, I mean. But can she come over now, too, if her mother says it's all right?"

"I guess so."

Abby picked up the receiver in the living room and dialed Potsie's apartment. The phone rang a long time. Finally Mrs. Torres answered.

Abby cleared her throat. "Hi, Mrs. Torres."

"You're up pretty late, Abby," she said.

"Is Potsie awake?"

"I'll see."

It seemed to take forever for Potsie to get to the phone, and when she did, it sounded as if she was almost asleep. "What's up?" she asked.

"You've got to come over here. Right away. Stay the night."

"Too late," Potsie said, yawning. "I'm almost asleep."

"Potsie," Abby said. "I think I left my memo book in the closet in apartment 2B." She swallowed, thinking of Garcia. "My name is all over it. Maybe I could go to jail."

Potsie gasped. "We'll have to get it back," she said. "Tomorrow. First thing."

"Not tomorrow. Tonight. After midnight. Before someone finds it. Come with me."

"Me?" Potsie squeaked. "I don't even like to go to the bathroom in the dark . . ." She broke off and began again. "You're right. Let me ask my mother."

Three minutes later she was back. "Abby, I'm really sorry. She said no with a capital N. She thinks we'll be up all night."

"I'll have to go alone," Abby said.

"Don't do it. Wait . . ."

"Listen, Potsie. There's nothing to it." She giggled nervously. "If I'm still alive you can come over for dinner tomorrow night. Eggie said so."

She hung up and went back into her bedroom. For a while she walked around trying to stay awake. Every few minutes she listened next to the wall. Once she thought she heard something rustle on the other side, but she couldn't be sure.

She sank down on the edge of the bed. She was so tired that her eyes kept closing. She could hear music in the living room. Eggie was listening to the Golden Oldies. Dan was probably in his room.

She reached for the clock and set it for two o'clock.

When the alarm jangled three hours later, she awoke with a start. She fumbled with the clock to turn it off, swung her legs over the side of the bed, and tiptoed out of the apartment.

She moved down the shadowy hall toward the door to 2B, wondering if the door was still open and hoping that whoever was in the apartment was sound asleep.

She was almost sorry when she spotted the matchbook cover still sticking out of the edge of the door like a little pink flag. It seemed odd that no one had seen it there all day.

Slowly she pushed the door open with the palm of her hand and caught the matchbook as it fell. It was so dark in the apartment that she couldn't see anything. For a moment she stood there listening, but there wasn't a sound.

She stepped into the apartment and drew the door shut behind her. It closed with a little click. She strained forward, listening, but no one seemed to have heard.

She inched her way along, her heart beating wildly, holding on to the wall. She edged one foot in front of the other, ready to stop if anything creaked. The floor felt cold and gritty under her bare feet and her bathrobe made a funny little swishing sound against the floor. She tried to swallow but her mouth was too dry. She grabbed up her robe and felt for the molding around the closet.

When she reached it, she groped around blindly for the knob and swung the door open. She dropped to her knees and ran her hand along the dusty floor until she felt the cardboard cover of her pad. She scooped it up and stuck it in her bathrobe pocket.

As she stood up, she bumped her head on a wire coathanger, but before she could grab it it, clattered to the floor.

She waited, frozen, for something to happen. But nothing did. After the noise from the coat hanger died away, the apartment was as silent as ever.

By this time, it didn't seem quite as dark. Abby could see faint outlines in the kitchen at the end of the hallway, the square shapes of the stove and the refrigerator. A glow, probably from the streetlamp outside, made a dim patch of gray in the hallway.

She wondered what was in that bedroom. The door was open, just as she'd left it. She stood there undecided. Should she risk a look? She waited until her heart stopped beating so fast, then, silently, she took two or three steps toward the bedroom and peeked around the edge of the door.

The streetlights shone on a small, dusty-looking table lamp, its shade torn and tilted to one side. A cup stood on the windowsill.

She leaned in a little farther, trying to see in the darkness. Her shoulder grazed the light switch.

The ceiling light in the bedroom went on. At the same moment there was an explosion of sound.

Abby stood frozen as the bedroom lamp teetered and crashed to the floor and a voice began to screech at her.

CHAPTER 12

"Go away," Abby mumbled to Eggie the next morning. She pulled the covers up over her head.

"Potsie's on the phone," Eggie said. "She says she has to talk to you."

Abby stumbled out of bed and padded down the hall in her bare feet.

"Potsie," she said into the phone, "I'm okay, but get over here right away. There are so many mysteries going on, I don't know where to begin." She clunked down the phone and raced back into her bedroom for her clothes.

Ten minutes later, she was outside the front door of the apartment, still buttoning her sweater. "Don't let Eggie hear us," she whispered to Potsie when she came up. "We have to get over to 2B."

They tiptoed across the hall. "Wait till you see . . ." Abby began, and suddenly stopped.

"Potsie! The pink matchbook is gone."

"Gone?"

"It was here at three o'clock this morning. I know because I put it back in the door when I left the apartment. Someone had to have opened the door since then because the matchbook isn't here."

"Will you please tell me what's going on?"

"Let's get out of here first," Abby said. "We'll sit on the stairway out of sight. We'll be able to see if anyone comes out of the apartment."

"What happened?" Potsie asked as they sank down on the third step from the top. "I can't wait another minute."

"I was in the apartment—in the hall," Abby began, "and I leaned on the light switch by accident. The whole bedroom lit up like the Fourth of July."

Potsie leaned forward.

"I woke him up. Or her."

"Abby!" Potsie groaned.

"There was a noise. Whirring. Feathers flying around."

"A bird?" Potsie asked, a little disappointed.

"Not an ordinary bird. A huge bird. Almost as long as my arm. He's bright blue and has big blue eyes"— Abby made circles in the air with her index fingers— "all ringed with yellow. And there's yellow around his beak."

"But you said that whatever was in there was calling you names."

Abby nodded. "He keeps turning his head to one

side and saying . . ." She paused, and said in a harsh voice, "R-i-i-p." She shrugged. "I thought he was saying, 'Drip.'"

"But what is a bird doing sitting by itself in the middle of apartment 2B?"

"I don't know, but someone is feeding it. There's a mess of cereal or something in a bowl in the kitchen and some bits of eggs. And there's a cup on the windowsill in the bedroom. It's probably filled with . . ."

"What's that?" Potsie interrupted. "I thought I heard a click."

Abby stood up and popped her head around the corridor wall. "Look, Potsie, someone must have just come out of 2B," she whispered.

"How can you tell?"

"I think I saw a shadow move across the hall. . . ."

"Maybe he's going downstairs. Waiting for the elevator. Let's take a look."

Abby jumped up. "You're right. We'll take the stairs. Beat the elevator. See who comes out."

They raced down the stairs, listening to the clank of the elevator as it descended slowly behind them. They reached the front vestibule as the elevator came to a stop on the first floor.

The doors slid open. Out stepped Mrs. Krumback. She was talking to Kiki. They had a shopping cart between them. They were probably going to the supermarket.

In back of the Krumbacks was Abby's brother, Dan. He was lugging two large cans of paint. Some of the paint had slopped over the side of one can, leaving a blotch of purple on the outside.

Dan looked toward the vestibule. When he saw Abby and Potsie, he got back into the elevator. A moment later, the doors closed and the elevator went up.

"Why did he do that?" Potsie asked.

"I have to talk to you about Dan, Potsie."

"Come on," Potsie said. "I have a half hour before my dentist appointment and I just got my allowance. Let's get a soda. You can tell me all about it."

Abby followed her out of the lobby and down the street to Coco's. They walked to the back and sat down at one of the booths.

"What'll it be, girls?" the waitress asked.

"Coke," Potsie said.

"Two." Abby pulled a napkin out of the holder and began to fold it into strips. "Dan's in trouble," she told Potsie as the waitress went back to the counter. "I know it. Garcia told me one time to watch when people start to do things differently. Well, Dan is doing something different, all right. He's locking his bedroom door. He's walking around with strange packages. And guess what it said on the package?" She took a deep breath. "H. M."

"His initials?"

"Don't be dumb. His are D.J. Don't you get it? H. M. Hyacinth Macaw."

Potsie nodded slowly.

"And worse yet, Potsie. I heard Witkowski on the phone. I'm pretty sure the robbery took place in the pet shop."

Potsie's mouth opened in a little round circle. "Do you think Dan . . ."

"I don't know." Absently she reached for the Coke that the waitress put on the table. She took a long sip. "Another thing. A girl called him last night. I heard him planning something for tonight with her."

"Do you think it was Hyacinth?"

"Probably. They might be ready to take a plane. Go to South America. They've got enough money if they stole two thousand dollars." She shrugged. "Who knows what they're up to? We'll have to watch him every minute after supper. In the meantime, I think I can get the key for his room. We'd better check out any clues we find, maybe find out Hyacinth's address and persuade her to go back home." She took another sip.

Potsie sat up straight. "Listen, Abby. I know I haven't been much help. I'm always scared of everything." She licked her lips. "But now that your brother is involved, I'm really going to try harder. Get into the spirit. Maybe we'll get a medal for capturing him."

"Potsie! Are you crazy?"

Potsie clapped her hand over her mouth.

Abby gulped down the rest of her drink. "Let's go."

They stood up. "There's something else that's been bothering me all morning," Abby said, "that feeling of gravel on the floor of 2B."

"Birdseed?"

Abby stared at her. "You're right. Birdseed. But I felt it somewhere else. Just the other day. But where?"

Potsie left the money on the table and they walked

out of the diner. They started up Washington Avenue, Abby still trying to remember.

Suddenly she grabbed Potsie's arm. "I know. That gritty stuff was on Dan's bedroom floor."

"He's got something to do with the bird, then."

"Of course. He probably stole it." She gulped. "Too."

Potsie shook her head. "I can't believe it."

Abby leaned against the telephone pole. "I can't, either. But the evidence points to him. It seems that he's turned into a regular thief."

CHAPTER 13

On the corner a man was giving balloons away. He pumped one full of helium for a little girl. The black marks on an orange balloon became letters and grew larger.

They said:

DON'T IGNORE
JUSTINE'S NEW STORE.

"Hah!" said Abby. "That's the place that doesn't like children."

"Pretty dumb to give out balloons, then," Potsie said.

"Crazy." Abby waved good-bye to Potsie and wandered across the street to sit on her steps while Potsie went to the dentist. The sun had gone behind a cloud. She folded her arms across her chest and shivered. It was really too cold to sit there, she thought, but she didn't feel like going back upstairs. Eggie would probably ask her to do dishes or make her bed.

Behind her, the door opened. "Abby, will you get off those steps," Mrs. Krumback called out irritably. "Nobody can get in here without falling all over your feet."

Slowly Abby stood up. She moved to the side of the building and leaned back against the brick wall.

Dan came out. This time he was carrying a brown paper bag. Even though he almost stepped on her feet, he didn't seem to notice her.

"Dummy," she muttered, and watched him cross the street and go into Elmo's Hardware Store on the corner.

She hesitated, trying to decide whether she should follow him or go upstairs and try to get into his room. She had no idea how long he would stay out. And if he caught her in his room—she sighed, then walked slowly across the street and went into the hardware store.

Dan was standing at the counter talking to Elmo. "I didn't need as much as I thought," Dan was saying. "I didn't even open this can. Can I get my money back?"

Elmo bent over and checked the can. He looked a little annoyed, Abby thought, as she tiptoed toward them.

"I guess it's all right," Elmo said.

"What are you painting?" she asked, leaning over Dan's shoulder.

She could feel him jump. "How did you get here?"

"I want to talk to you."

"I want to talk to you, too," he said. "Did you see my wallet?"

"It was on the kitchen table last night," she said, thinking that anyone who couldn't even look as far as under the living room couch didn't deserve to find it. She lowered her voice. "Come on outside. I want to talk to you and I don't want the whole world to hear."

Dan held out his hand for the money, and Elmo slapped it on the counter. Dan scooped up the money, then sauntered out of the store.

Abby marched after him. "Listen, Dan." She took a deep breath. "Do you know what will happen . . ."

"Hurry up, will you, Abby. I've got stuff to do upstairs."

"What stuff?"

Dan sighed. "Do you have to know everything?"

She put her hands on her hips. "I do know everything."

Dan looked around. "Then don't tell anybody. I've really got a good thing going."

Abby looked up at him. A skinny line of purple paint was stuck to one of his ears. He didn't look guilty, she thought. She stood there, not sure of what to say.

Before she could make up her mind, Dan hurried

away from her. "Remember," he said, "don't tell anybody. You'll spoil all my plans."

"You're going to end up in jail," she yelled after him.

There was so much traffic in the street, he probably
couldn't hear her, she thought. But she kept yelling
anyway. "You have no right to do this to me. Suppose
Garcia finds out," she shouted as he disappeared into
the apartment house.

She made a face at a woman who was staring at her,
then went down the street to look into the pet-shop
window until the woman had crossed the street.

A moment later, Potsie appeared next to her. "Great
news," she said. "The dentist has the flu."

Abby tried to smile. "You know, Potsie, I think it's
time I took a look at Dan's bedroom."

"Search it?"

She nodded. "Maybe we'll get some clues. We've got
to stop him."

They took the elevator upstairs to the apartment.
Eggie was in the kitchen. "Staying for dinner tonight?"
she asked Potsie. "That's good. I dreamed of pot roast
last night and that probably means the dinner will
come out terrific tonight."

She held out a plate of cookies. "Good thing you two
came around now. I'm eating my way through these."

"Have you seen Dan?" Abby asked, taking the larg-
est cookie she could find.

"He's in his bedroom, I think."

"Don't you think he should get some fresh air?"
Abby asked. "I could tell him you said so."

Mrs. Eggler shook her head. "It's not that warm out."

Abby motioned to Potsie. "See you later, Eggie. We'll be in my room."

Abby marched down the hall. "Maybe we can get rid of him ourselves."

"How?"

"Watch." She opened the front door quietly, rang the bell, and shut the door again. "I'll get it," she yelled. She banged open the door. "He's in his bedroom," she said to the empty hall. "Yes. I'll tell him."

She slammed the door.

A moment later, Dan appeared at the other end of the hallway.

"Was that for me?" he asked.

"It was someone from your class. I don't remember his name." She crossed her fingers behind her back. "He was in a hurry. He said he'd meet you at the park."

"When?"

"Now. Hurry up. He wants to play ball."

Dan stood there for a moment thinking. "I have to go to work soon," he said. Then he disappeared into his bedroom and came running out with his jacket over his arm. "Going to the park, and then to work," he shouted in at Eggie, and slammed the door.

"Excellent," Abby said. "Now let's make sure he's really gone."

They raced into her bedroom and looked out the

window. "It'll take him a minute to get down the street," Abby said.

"There he goes," Potsie said. "Running along like a rabbit."

They grinned at each other.

"But how are you going to explain when he gets back?" Potsie asked.

Abby waved her hand in the air. "There should be someone at the park. He'll start to play ball and forget the whole thing. Come on." She tiptoed into the living room and knelt next to the couch. "You can see what a spectacular housekeeper Eggie is," she said as she pulled out Dan's wallet.

She opened the wallet and grinned up at Potsie. "Just as I suspected. Here's the key. Let's hurry up. If Dan changes his mind and comes back, he'll kill me if he sees me in his room."

They raced down the hall. Abby turned the key in Dan's lock and nodded. "Fits." She gave the knob a push. "Let's search this place from top to bottom, as we investigators say."

"Ye-ucks," Potsie said, looking into Dan's room over Abby's shoulder.

"If my mother saw this room," Abby said, "it would be the end of Dan." She kicked at a wad of crumpled-up brown paper, then bent down and picked it up. "See these initials? H.M." She rubbed her foot against the floor. "And do you see what I mean about this floor? All gritty or sandy or something."

Potsie nodded. "It's birdseed, all right. Or gravel."

Abby went over to the closet. Dan's blanket still lay there, covering the bulky package. She yanked the blanket out of the way and stepped back.

For a moment there was silence as they stared at the object in the corner of the closet. It was a large granite birdbath, chipped and moldy-looking, with a long crack running down one side. A stone pigeon, its head spattered with a greenish stain, perched on its edge. On one side was a section for seed. It was about half full.

"That's the ugliest thing I've ever seen," Potsie said. "It looks as if a lot of birds have used it."

"Probably thousands," Abby said. She made a face. "How did he ever lug this thing all the way up here?"

"And why?"

"That part's easy. To give his friend, the bird in 2B, a bath." She tried to smile. "What a disgrace. Here I am, practically a detective, and I have a criminal in my own apartment." She looked around. "I wonder if he took that two thousand dollars? It could be anywhere."

Potsie fished in her pocket and pulled out a crumpled pack of gum. "Here," she said, "take a stick and calm down."

Abby took the pack absently. "We've got to take the bird back," she said as she stuffed two sticks into her mouth. She chewed for a moment, thinking how angry she was at him.

"Back?"

"To the pet store, of course. Don't you see, Potsie? The bird comes from the pet store." She shook her head. "This is getting worse and worse. Who knows how many things Dan's stolen?"

FROM THE MEMO BOOK OF
JENNIFER A. JONES

DATE: Thursday, April 8.
TIME: Afternoon.

HOW TO SAVE DANIEL JONES.
1. Take bird back.
2. Find out what happens tonight. Follow.
3. Find out if he took two thou.
4. If so, grab. Bring back. NO. SEND BACK IN ENVELOPE.
5. Find any other stuff. Give back. (Or throw away if real junk.)
6. GET DAN AWAY FROM H.M. SHE IS A TERRIBLE INFLUENCE.

CHAPTER 14

It had started to rain. Big drops splattered against Abby's bedroom window. She lay sprawled on her bed eating an apple and looking at the street reflected in her dresser mirror. Potsie was stretched out on the floor.

"As soon as the pet shop closes," Abby said, "we can dash right over to 2B, grab the bird, and . . ."

Potsie looked up. "I hope the door to 2B is still open."

Abby stared at her. "That door had better be open. I can't go down that fire escape again in this weather."

Abby aimed the apple core at her wastebasket. It hit the rim, then landed against the wall with a thud and dropped to the floor. "I can't imagine," she said slowly, "why Dan has that picture of Queen Victoria in that fat gold frame."

"What got me," Potsie said, "were the purple earrings painted on it."

"Do you suppose the initials H.M. on the outside of the package were for Her Majesty instead of Hyacinth Macaw?" Abby walked across the room and threw the apple into the wastebasket and rubbed at the stain on the yellow wallpaper. "Do you think my brother's insane?" she asked. "It's going to be an awful jolt for my mother if he is."

"Listen, Abby, I wouldn't worry about that for one minute. There are lots of crazy people walking around in this world. Nobody minds at all."

"I guess so," Abby answered a little doubtfully. She looked at the clock on her dresser. We have about ten minutes before the pet shop closes. What do you say we get over to 2B now? See if the door is still open."

Potsie stood up. "I'm dying to get a look at the bird. But I've been wondering, Abby. Suppose Dan comes over to 2B right after work. Now that we know he's . . ." She paused and tapped her head. "He might do anything."

"A minute ago, you weren't worried," Abby said. "Well, I don't think he'll throw us out the window or strangle us or . . ."

Potsie held up her hand. "Stop. I don't want to get myself nervous."

Abby laughed. "Don't be silly. Dan couldn't hurt a flea." She frowned. "I think." She stood up, too. "Anyway, I think you're right. We'd better get out of 2B before he comes home." She picked up her raincoat. "Come on. Let's go see Jack."

Potsie raised her eyebrows.

"That's what I call the bird." She threw her raincoat over her shoulders.

With Potsie three steps behind her, Abby yelled good-bye to Eggie and rushed out of the door before Eggie could ask where they were going.

The door to apartment 2B was open. "All that worry for nothing," Abby said.

They stepped inside. She bent down and picked up the pink matchbook cover. She nodded. "Someone was in here, all right." She tucked the matchbook in her pocket. "We'll leave it in the door again when we go out."

"For what? The bird will be gone."

"I may want to get in again," Abby said. "I'd love to be here when Dan sees that the bird has"—she waved her hands over her head—"flown the coop."

Together they went down the hall and peered through the open bedroom door. The bird was perched on the top of an old cane chair.

"He's beautiful," Potsie breathed. "That blue is so bright."

Abby nodded. "I told you, didn't I?" Slowly she walked into the room. "You wouldn't hurt me, would you?" she asked the bird, watching his curved beak and the powerful talons that gripped the chair.

Almost in answer the bird spread one wing lazily, stretched, and folded his wing over his body. "R-i-i-p," he said in a hoarse voice.

"Do you think he's friendly?" Potsie asked a little nervously.

Abby shook her head. "I don't know. After I took a quick look at him last night, I raced back to bed. Right now I'm going into the kitchen to see if I can find something for him to eat. Make friends that way."

Abby turned and took a step. There was a great whir of feathers. The bird flew off his perch and sailed out of the room behind her. Instinctively she ducked and threw her arms up to protect her face.

The bird landed on her head.

Abby shrieked. "Get him off," she yelled to Potsie.

"Shoo," Potsie said. She backed up against the hall wall. "Shoo."

Abby swatted at the bird with her hand. He rocked back and forth on her head trying to keep his balance, then grasped her shoulder gently with one cool, black talon. Abby stood there quietly until he transferred himself from her head to her shoulder.

"Potsie, you idiot," she said out of the corner of her mouth. "It's a good thing this bird turned out to be friendly. For all the help you are, he might have ripped me to pieces."

"I'm a terrible coward," Potsie said.

"Never mind that now," Abby said. She watched the bird. Head cocked, he teetered on her shoulder and stared at her with one gold-rimmed eye. "Something I never thought of, Pots," she said absently. "How are we going to get this bird across the street to the pet shop? He may fly off my shoulder any minute and we might not be able to catch him again."

At the other end of the hall there was a noise.

Abby looked up. "What's that?"

She stared fascinated as the door to the apartment opened slowly and someone began to push a box inside.

She motioned violently to Potsie, and dashed into the kitchen with the bird hanging on to her shoulder. "Out the fire escape," she mouthed. "Hurry."

As Potsie shoved up the window, Abby yanked the tablecloth off the kitchen table and tossed it over the bird and the top of her head.

"I can't go out there," Potsie moaned.

Behind them, in the hall, there were footsteps.

"Hurry," Abby whispered frantically. She gave Potsie a little shove.

Potsie rolled her eyes toward the hall and clambered out onto the fire escape.

"Come on, bird," Abby said. She put her leg over the sill and crawled out in back of Potsie.

CHAPTER 15

It was getting dark. The wind blew the rain against the apartment building. Abby could feel the window rattling behind her as she crouched in a corner of the fire escape. Water streamed from her hair. Next to her, Potsie, eyes squinched shut, was a sodden mess.

Abby peeked under a corner of the tablecloth. The bird seemed dry and perfectly contented as he gripped Abby's shoulder.

She shivered. "Open your eyes, Potsie, and look in the window. Try to see who's in there! Maybe it's Dan."

"I can't," Potsie answered. "I'm probably going to fall any minute."

Abby sighed and swiveled around as much as she could to peer through the apartment window. Under the bunched-up tablecloth, the bird shifted nervously on her shoulder.

The living-room light went on.

"I don't know if I can manage the fire-escape stairs with this bird," she told Potsie. "Besides, there are too many people walking around down there. They might see . . ."

"I can't even open my eyes," Potsie said, "much less go down those stairs."

"That settles it, then. We'll wait here until whoever is in the apartment goes away."

"Can you see anybody in there?"

Abby craned her neck. "No. Hey, the living-room light went out. We'll wait another minute or two and then . . ."

A drop of water rolled down her forehead. She wiped her face with one hand. "Never mind. We won't even wait a second. Open the window."

Potsie opened one eye, inched over to the window, and pushed it up. She scrambled in ahead of Abby and helped her in.

They stood there listening. "Gone," Abby said finally. She pulled the tablecloth off the bird. Clucking softly, the bird released his grip from Abby's shoulder and flew to the top of the refrigerator.

Abby rubbed her shoulder. "Am I glad to be rid of him. Come on, Pots. Let's check out that package."

A minute later they were kneeling on the living-room floor inspecting the large, flat parcel leaning against the wall.

"Only one way to find out," Abby said, looking at the brown wrapping paper that covered it. She flicked

the package with her finger, then picked at the edge with one nail.

"Do you think you should do that?" Potsie asked.

"I'll just peel the edge a little," Abby said. She tore a small piece of the brown paper off one corner and leaned over to get a closer look. "White," she said. "White canvas."

"A picture?" Potsie asked.

Abby ripped the brown paper a little further. "I don't know. It still looks white, but there's a blob of blue down there. I can't quite . . . Potsie, do you think Dan stole this, too?"

"If you tear it anymore you might as well open the whole thing," said Potsie nervously. "If we get caught, we're really going to get in a lot of trouble."

Abby snorted. "We're already in trouble. Did you forget that we've already broken into this apartment?" She gestured toward the kitchen with her thumb. "And that bird flying around in there is stolen goods, as they say in the detective bureau. What's one more thing like an opened package?"

She stood up reluctantly and glanced toward the window. "It's starting to get dark. We'd better take the bird back now." She nudged the package with her foot. "We can take a look at this later. Help me catch him and put the tablecloth over him again. Then we'll get out of here."

Ten minutes later, they huddled together at the back door of the pet shop. Abby pushed a strand of wet hair out of her eyes. "How could we be so stupid?"

she moaned. She shifted her arm to ease the weight of the bird. "I never thought about the door being locked. We could try the rest of the stores on the street. Maybe someone else left a door open. We could get in, go down the cellar, walk along . . ."

"Stop! It's bad enough that I'm standing here soaking wet. Now you're going to make me set off a bunch of burglar alarms and end up at the station house under arrest," Potsie said.

Abby squinted up at a window just over their heads. It was covered with heavy iron bars. "Look up there, Potsie. The window's open."

"What about the bars? We'd never squeeze through."

"We don't have to," Abby said. "Maybe we can get Jack up there. He's a lot skinnier than we are. I can open the window a speck more and push him through."

Potsie flicked a drop of rain off her eyelashes. "What about a cage? You can't let him loose in the pet shop all night."

"Why not? He's been flying around 2B all this time." Abby looked around. "Pull that crate over here, Potsie, and help me get up on it."

Potsie scurried down the alley and dragged a wooden box under the window. "It's full of gook," she complained, wiping her muddy fingers on her jeans.

Abby didn't answer. With one arm on Potsie's shoulder and her side braced against the building, she climbed up on the box. Under the tablecloth, the bird teetered on her arm.

"I don't think I can do this," she said, looking down

at Potsie. "I'll never be able to open the window and hold the bird, too."

"Move over a little," Potsie said. "I'm coming up. I won't fall, will I?"

Potsie stood frozen on the box for a moment, then she reached up and shoved the window open.

Carefully Abby turned her body until her shoulder was level with the sill. She let the tablecloth fall back so the bird could see. "Go ahead, Jack," she encouraged. "Climb right in. It's nice and warm inside. Dry, too."

For a moment longer, the bird stayed perched on Abby's shoulder. Then, daintily, he stepped onto the sill and ducked through the horizontal bars on the window into the store.

Abby peered inside as the bird sailed across the counter in the back and landed on top of a large cage full of gerbils. "R-i-i-p," he said, and began to preen his feathers.

Abby looked at Potsie. "What a relief," she said. "Let's get out of here. We're late for supper. And remember, we have to keep an eye on Dan. We have to see what's going to happen tonight."

They jumped off the box and tore down the alley, Abby a few steps ahead of Potsie.

As she turned out of the alley, she crashed right into Garcia. "Hey," he grinned. "What do I have here? You're wetter than a fish."

Mouth open, Abby tried to catch her breath. "What are you doing here?" she stammered.

He took her by the shoulders. "Don't be so frightened. It's only me. I was checking a couple of things out."

Abby inhaled deeply. "I guess I didn't expect to see you here."

Behind her, Potsie rounded the corner. "Garcia," she gasped.

Garcia looked from one to the other. "All right. What are you two up to?"

Abby's heart was beating so wildly now that she didn't even try to speak. She pictured Dan in jail, herself in disgrace. Maybe Garcia would never talk to her again.

"We're practicing to be detectives," Potsie said firmly, "involved in a case." She put her arm through Abby's. "We're a little late for supper, though."

From across the street, Witkowski called. "Come on, Garcia. We've got a call."

Garcia put up his hand and ran it through his curly hair. "Listen, girls," he said. "I don't want you running around in alleys this time of . . ."

"It's urgent," Witkowski yelled.

"I've got to go," Garcia said. "Why don't you go home now, too?"

"We're going right now," Abby promised.

As Garcia took off across the street, Potsie beamed at her. "That was close."

They crossed the street and headed for the apartment house. In the lobby they glanced toward the elevator but the arrow pointed to five. Rather than wait, they took the stairs two at a time and arrived at the front door as Eggie was opening it.

CHAPTER 16

Eggie stood there wearing a plaid raincoat and a green plastic hat with a floppy brim. "I was coming to look for you two," she said. "Dinner is going to be all cold and dried up."

Abby waved her hand in the air. "Don't worry. We like it all cold and dried up." She looked down the hall. "Is Dan here?"

"Of course, we've been waiting for you. Where have you been, anyway? The two of you are going to catch pneumonia walking around in the rain like that. Better get on something dry." Without waiting for an answer, Eggie clumped back into the kitchen muttering that she'd be cleaning up the kitchen half the night while the rest of the world watched television.

Abby motioned to Potsie. "Come on," she said. "I'll find you a pair of jeans or something."

Five minutes later, they rushed down the hall

toward the kitchen, Potsie in a pair of faded green pants and Abby in her pink robe. "We'll set the table, Eggie," Abby said.

Eggie met them at the kitchen door. "Never mind," she said. "It's all done."

In honor of Potsie's visit, Eggie had pushed the table into the center of the room. It was covered with an old red tablecloth and the best pink dishes. In the center was a pot of dusty ivy.

Abby gulped. "It certainly looks . . ."

"Colorful," Eggie finished for her. She tilted her head to one side. "Some people would say that pink and red don't go too well, but I always say anything different looks good."

Abby nodded, trying not to giggle.

In back of her, Dan came down the hall whistling. "Table looks great, Eggie," he said as he moved around Abby and slid into a chair.

Eggie smiled at him.

Abby frowned, wondering what Eggie would say if she ever found out that Dan was . . .

"My famous slumgullion," Eggie said in a loud voice. She hefted a large blue bowl onto the table. "I threw in the leftover stuffed cabbage."

Abby leaned over to look: chunks of stringy meat, a pile of noodles and rice stuck together, some carrots, and a gray piece of cabbage floating on congealed brown gravy.

"It looks great," she said.

"Wonderful," Potsie agreed.

"Well, I wouldn't go that far," Eggie said, "but it certainly beats hamburgers."

"That's true," Abby said. She spooned some of the slumgullion onto her plate. Eggie's hamburgers were the worst she had ever tasted. "By the way"—she pushed the bowl toward Potsie—"I think I'll get a lock for my room as soon as I get some money together."

"I don't blame you," Potsie said.

Abby glanced at Dan. He was shoving noodles into his mouth a mile a minute. She narrowed her eyes.

"I wonder whatever happened to that dollar I lost last year," she said.

For a moment there was silence. "Maybe it was stolen," Potsie said.

"Maybe it was lost," Dan said. "Abby loses a lot of stuff."

"Kind of careless, I guess," Eggie said.

"But honest," said Potsie.

Dan wiped a smear of gravy off his chin. "Big deal."

Abby felt a lump in her throat. Dan had probably been stealing things all along. She turned to look at Potsie and nodded her head slowly. "Yes, I think I'd better get a lock for my bedroom."

"Put a lock on that bedroom," Eggie said, "and no one will be able to get in there and clean. The place will be impossible in a week or two." She pointed to the bowl of slumgullion. "Have some more, Potsie. You eat about as much as a bird. There's practically nothing on your plate except that piece of cabbage."

"That's all right," Potsie said quickly. "I'm really not

too hungry, Eggie. I had a lot to eat today." She cleared her throat. "Extra cereal at breakfast. Snacks. Stuff like that."

"Speaking of bedrooms," Eggie said, "you're a good kid, Dan, but your bedroom is usually pretty bad. And now that you're locking it"—she speared a piece of meat from the bowl and put it in her mouth—"it's probably the worst."

Abby looked at Dan from under her eyebrows.

"You can get in there tomorrow," he said. "Dust all you want."

Abby stared down at her plate. He was going to get rid of all the things he had in there tonight. Fly to South America.

"Well, Dan," Eggie said, "how about a dream for us?"

Dan looked up at the ceiling. "I dreamed of a storm. A gale. The wind was howling. . . ."

Eggie looked at him, horrified. "Trouble," she said. "That means trouble."

"What kind of trouble?" Abby asked.

Dan laughed. "I'm not worried." He scraped back his chair. "There's a game on TV," he said. "I think I'll watch it for a little while."

"Don't you want dessert?" Eggie called after him.

Dan didn't answer. A moment later, they heard him turn on the television in the living room.

Abby put down her fork and shoved her plate away. "I'll be right back," she said slowly. "I just want to talk to Dan about something."

Potsie nodded. "Good idea."

"Doesn't anyone want any pie?" Eggie asked. "It's probably defrosted by now."

"I do," Potsie answered. "I'll have a piece while I wait for Abby. I'll help with the dishes, too, if you want."

Abby tiptoed into the living room.

Dan was crouched in front of the television watching a baseball game.

Abby cleared her throat. "Dan, did you really dream that? About the wind and the gale?"

Dan nodded, hardly paying attention, as he turned up the volume on the television.

"Aren't you worried? Doesn't it make you think that you'd better not . . ."

He looked up. "Listen, Abby. I'm trying to watch this."

"But suppose Eggie's right?"

"Suppose Eggie's wrong?"

"Hey, will you turn down the television," she said irritably. "I can't hear myself think."

Dan turned his head. "Was that the doorbell?"

"I didn't hear anything. Dan, you know I want to be a detective someday. And what about Mother? And Daddy? And Garcia? What kind of a reputation will I have with a brother who's . . ."

"It *is* the doorbell," Dan said.

Abby sighed. "Never mind. I can't talk to you with the television blaring like that anyway." She hurried down the hall and threw open the front door.

There stood Hyacinth Macaw. Today she was wearing a red shirt that said: HOLLY BY GOLLY. "Is Daniel there?" she asked.

Mouth open, Abby stepped back.

The girl looked at her. "Is Daniel there?" she asked again.

CHAPTER 17

Abby ducked behind the open door to hide as much of her bathrobe as she could. "Daniel?" she repeated.

Hyacinth was taller than Abby remembered. Tall and skinny. "Daniel," the girl said firmly. She pushed back her hair with one long red nail.

"Come on in." Abby pulled the bottom of her robe together nervously. "Don't you live around here somewhere? I think I've seen you before. But I can't exactly remember. . . ."

Hyacinth looked at her coolly. "On the subway. With that kid in her bare feet."

"Uhm, yes," Abby said. "I take the subway a lot. Every day." She glanced back over her shoulder toward the living room. Dan was still watching the game. She tried to think of the right questions, the kind Garcia would ask.

"I think I saw you on Washington Avenue," Abby said at last.

The girl shrugged.

"By the telephone pole," Abby said pointedly.

"Is Daniel home or . . ." the girl asked.

"Ripping a sign down."

The girl shifted from one foot to the other. "I'm in a hurry."

"Just tell me why you tore the sign off the pole," Abby said, thinking that Garcia would never have come right out and asked that question.

Dan poked his head out of the living room as the girl opened her mouth. "Who was that?" he yelled, and broke off. "Hey," he said as he spotted her. "I didn't know you were here. Where's the dolly?"

"Out in the hall. I had a hard time getting it, but I finally talked my super into it. He said the last time I took it, we brought it back with bird goo all over it." She leaned around the edge of the door and pulled in a small loading-cart on wheels.

"Bring it in here," Dan said.

Hyacinth jerked her head for Abby to get out of the way, then gave the cart a push. With a screech of wheels it rolled down the hall.

At the same time Potsie came out of the kitchen. A thin line of purple ringed her mouth. "I finished the pie," she said.

"Blueberry?" Abby asked.

Potsie shook her head. "Raspberry."

Abby gestured toward the bedroom. "Guess who . . ."

A grating sound came from the bedroom. "Watch out," they heard Dan yell.

"Don't worry," Hyacinth answered. "I've got it."

As Abby tiptoed toward the bedroom, the door opened. Dan led the way, pulling the cart by a rope. Hyacinth guided it from behind.

Abby's eyes widened. On the cart, only partially hidden by the blanket, was the birdbath. And lying flat across the top was the painting of Queen Victoria.

"Wow," whispered Potsie in an awed voice.

Abby nodded slowly. The birdbath they had seen this morning had changed completely. No longer was it a dull gray stone spattered with green stains. Someone had covered it with bright purple paint.

It was horrible.

"Out of the way, Abby," Dan shouted as he dragged the cart down the hall toward the door.

"What's going on?" Abby asked. "Where did you get that?"

Dan dropped the rope and scratched at the purple paint on his ear. "As a matter of fact, some old lady sold it to me for a dollar. It's an investment, you might say." He turned to the girl. "Hold on to that, Holly, while I open the door."

He fumbled with the knob.

Abby stared at her. "Holly? That's a funny nickname for Hyacinth," she said.

Dan opened the door and picked up the rope.

"What are you talking about?" Hyacinth asked. She maneuvered the back end of the cart through the open doorway. "My name is Holly." She reached for the door to close it behind her. "Holly," she said again. "Holly Monk."

The door shut with a bang. The sound echoed through the hall. Then there was silence. Abby and Potsie looked at each other. "Holly Monk," they said together.

"Who on earth, then," asked Abby, "is Hyacinth Macaw?"

Potsie shook her head.

"We'll have to figure that out later," Abby said, "but right now we're letting Dan and that girl get away. Let's see what they're up to." She ran into her bedroom and grabbed her raincoat.

As she came back into the hall, she tucked up her bathrobe in great bunches under the raincoat. "I guess this won't stay very well," she said, "but it's the best I can do."

Eggie appeared in the kitchen doorway, newspaper in her hand. "I don't seem to be getting much help with the dishes," she said.

Quickly Abby tucked in the loop of her bathrobe belt and covered it with her raincoat. "We'll be right back, Eggie," she said as casually as she could. "Then we'll help."

"It's almost eight o'clock," Eggie said.

Abby opened the door. "Don't worry. We're just going down on the avenue." She raised her eyebrows behind Eggie's back and headed for the stairs.

"No more than a half hour," Eggie called after them.

"All right," Abby said, and rushed down the stairs after Potsie.

"Good thing they won't be able to move too fast with that birdbath," she said, panting.

At the outside door they hesitated. Potsie pointed. "There they go, crossing the street, holding up traffic."

They ran down the avenue until they had almost caught up, then slowed down so they could stay about a block behind Dan and the girl. Every once in a while, Abby stopped to bunch up her bathrobe, then ran to catch up to Potsie.

At I Street, Abby pointed. "This is where I thought Hyacinth was hiding out." They went another block. On J Street Dan and the girl stopped. They stood talking for a moment, then trundled the cart into a store around the corner.

"Come on, Pots," Abby said, walking faster. "I can't see which store. . . . Do you suppose he's trying to sell that birdbath?"

"Insane," Potsie said.

Abby and Potsie stopped at the corner and leaned on the mailbox. "Whew," Potsie said. "I thought we'd be walking all night."

"Look, Pots, it must be that new store." Together they stared at a big sign over the doorway: JUSTINE'S JUNKTIQUES.

"The one that doesn't like children," Potsie said.

They watched Dan and the girl through the lighted store-window talking to a fat woman with lots of curly blond hair. Then the three of them walked toward the back of the store.

"That must be Justine," Abby said. "Let's get up closer and see what's going on. Just be careful they don't see us."

They waited for the light to change, then crossed J Street and peered through the window. "Junktiques is right," Potsie snorted. "I never saw such a mess of stuff in my life. I bet it's the only place in the world that would want something like that birdbath."

"And," Abby said, "a picture of Queen Victoria with earrings . . ." She nudged Potsie. "Look at that sign."

JUSTINE'S ART CONTEST
CASH PRIZE FOR THE MOST
ORIGINAL JUNKTIQUE
THURSDAY NIGHT, APRIL 8
NOTE: CHILDREN WELCOME.

Abby drew in her breath. "Children welcome," she said. "I can't believe it."

Potsie nodded. "The other sign was wet, remember, and part of it was missing."

Abby stood there thinking. "Potsie, you idiot. What did you tell me that girl's name was? The one who broke the window with Dan?"

"Howie said her name was Priest or something like that."

Abby raised her eyebrows. "What's another name for Priest?"

Potsie gasped. "I must have had the names mixed up. He probably said Monk."

"Holly Monk," Abby said slowly. "They're partners, I bet. Not only did they steal that money but now they're trying to win a prize to pay for Peter Tanner's window or maybe fly to South America."

Suddenly she clutched Potsie's arm. "Good grief, Potsie. Look."

There, taped neatly in the corner of the window, was a sign.

HAVE YOU SEEN
A HYACINTH MACAW?
SUBSTANTIAL REWARD: $100.00
Telephone Justine 555-9442
Call Anytime Day or Night
Owner Heartbroken

Underneath the sign was a photograph of Justine. Her blond hair hung down around her neck in ringlets.

"What's that on her shoulder?" Potsie asked. "Could that be . . ."

Abby leaned a little closer. "Old Jack himself," she said.

"You mean," said Potsie, "old Hyacinth Macaw. Our bird."

"And look what it says underneath. THE HYA-CINTH MACAW IS AN EXOTIC BIRD FROM THE TROPICS. IT IS WORTH MORE THAN $2000.00."

"Two thousand!" Abby said. They stared at each

other. "Not a girl's name at all. The name of a bird. That's why Witkowski said pet. Not pet store. Pet. The bird."

Potsie nodded. "That's why Holly Monk tore those signs down. Either she was looking for Hyacinth herself—trying to get the hundred dollars—"

"Or," said Abby, "she was trying to keep people from looking for the bird."

"Anyway, the reward is ours. We can bring the bird back. And if Dan doesn't win the prize we can lend him the money for Mr. Tanner's window and probably still have a lot left over. Pizza every day. All the phone calls we want: Hawaii, China . . ."

Potsie's mouth opened. "Abby. The reward. It isn't ours yet."

Abby's eyes widened. She looked at Potsie in horror. "We just locked Hyacinth Macaw up in the pet shop. We'll have to get him out right away. Tonight." She shook her head. "And even then," she said slowly, "we won't get the reward."

"Why not?"

"How can I take a reward for something my brother's stolen? We'll be lucky if he doesn't go to jail."

CHAPTER 18

Most of the stores were closed now and there were only a few patches of light along Washington Avenue as they sped down the dark streets.

"How are we ever going to get that bird out of there?" Potsie said.

"We'll have to lure him out the window somehow," Abby answered between breaths. "Maybe . . ." She stopped running. "Stitch in my side.

"Maybe," she began again, "we could get some food. I think there was some of that gop he eats on the windowsill in 2B. We could stop there and . . ."

Potsie nodded. "Hurry."

A few minutes later, they raced through the vestibule into the elevator and waited impatiently to get out on the second floor.

The doors opened and Abby dashed down the corridor. Without hesitating she pushed open the door to 2B and stopped short.

Someone was in the living room.

Back toward them, in a hooded brown raincoat, a bulky figure knelt on the living-room floor looking at the brown paper parcel.

Abby gulped and started to back out of the apartment. She collided with Potsie, who was right behind her.

By the time she caught her breath, the figure had jumped up, grabbed the package, and barreled past them.

"Who? What?" Potsie gasped.

Abby stood there looking toward the door. "That wasn't Dan," she said.

"And it wasn't Holly," said Potsie.

"I'll bet I know who it was," Abby said slowly. "We can check it out later. And if I'm right, it means that Dan is innocent. And we can collect the reward. But right now, we have to try to get that bird!"

In the kitchen they found a small glass bowl on the table. Abby picked it up and sniffed at it. "Mashed banana with a bunch of seeds on it."

"Just the thing," Potsie said. "Let's go."

By the time they crossed the street it had stopped raining. A sliver of moon gleamed on the puddles and lighted the alley. At the other end a large truck was parked. Two men were unloading boxes.

Abby and Potsie waited until the men had carried a

package into one of the stores, then scurried down the alley, staying close to the buildings.

The crate was still in front of the pet-store window. Abby climbed up. "We've got to hurry," she whispered. "It's bright as day back here and any minute those men might come out."

"Don't waste time," Potsie answered nervously.

Abby leaned over and peered through the window. "Here, Jack." She tapped lightly on the crossbars. "Here, boy. Here, Hyacinth."

"Can you see him?" Potsie asked. "Do you want me to come up?"

"Yes. No. I mean that idiot bird is looking right at me." She clinked the bowl against the brick ledge. "Here, boy," she said again. "Nice mashed banana."

"Is he coming?"

"No."

Potsie reached up and grabbed Abby's jacket. Then she hopped up on the crate. "Maybe I could whistle a little."

"Watch out," Abby whispered urgently. "Here come the men again." She pulled Potsie back against the wall.

They waited for what seemed to be a long time while the men climbed into the truck and dragged out another box.

As soon as the men had disappeared into the building again, Potsie began to whistle. "I think he's coming, Abby," she said.

They watched as the bird took mincing steps across

the top of the birdcages. Several times he stopped and swiveled his head around to stare at them.

"Come on, old boy," Abby said. "Come get your din-din." She shoved the bowl sideways through the bars and waved it around.

"R-i-i-p," clucked the bird, and flew toward them. Slowly Abby drew the bowl outside. Jack ducked his head through the window bars and Potsie lunged for him.

The bird squawked as she pulled him out gently.

"Got him," Potsie yelled. "That's one hundred dollars right in our pockets."

"Ssh. Almost in our pockets," Abby said. "Hey, what's that noise?" She glanced toward the truck but the men were still inside the building.

"Come on, Pots." Abby jumped off the crate. With Potsie and the bird behind her, she went down the alley, circled around the parked truck, and dashed out on Washington Avenue.

"One thing nice about this bird," Abby said as they stopped at the corner to catch their breath, "he doesn't seem to mind being jounced all over the place."

"He's heavy, though," Potsie said. "You take him for a while."

Together they crossed the avenue and walked toward Justine's.

Ten minutes later they stood on the corner of Washington and J Street. Light from the Junktique Shop spilled out onto the street.

"Come on, Potsie," Abby said. "Look at all the people." She shouldered her way inside.

On a long counter in the front were a row of paint-
ings. And next to the counter was Dan's purple birdbath. Up toward the front, Abby spotted Dan and
Holly Monk. Nearby stood Kiki Krumback with her
mother. Kiki's red hair was wound around her head in
a fat braid, and Mrs. Krumback had taken her hair out
of the little pink rollers. Justine was standing to one
side writing something on a pad.

Abby cleared her throat. "Justine," she called, and
made her way through the crowd of people to the
front of the room.

Justine looked up. "Lulu," she shouted as she
spotted the hyacinth macaw.

"Edgar," yelled Kiki Krumback.

With a whir of feathers, the bird flew into the air
and landed on Justine's shoulder. "You found my bird,"
Justine said. "You found my Lulu."

"What a relief," said Kiki Krumback, pushing her
braid forward. "I thought Edgar had flown south."

"Edgar?" Justine asked, her voice rising.

Kiki shrugged. "He looks like an Edgar to me."

"I was right," Abby whispered to Potsie. "Kiki
Krumback stole the bird."

"How did you know?" asked Potsie.

"The painting in 2B. Remember we saw a piece of
blue on the canvas? It reminded me of the bird. And
then when we saw someone in the apartment, it just
clicked. Kiki Krumback is an artist. She was sure to
enter the contest. And she was using Justine's own bird
hoping she'd win a prize."

Justine was laughing and crying at the same time as

the bird leaned over her shoulder and pecked gently at her cheek.

"I'm sorry," Kiki said to Justine. "I never meant you to worry. I figured you wouldn't mind if I borrowed him for a couple of days. I kept him in an empty apartment so my cat wouldn't hurt him. And I left a note in the top drawer of that dresser you have in the window."

"You mean that one with the mirror on top?"
Kiki nodded.

"That was sold days ago. I never saw a note."

Potsie leaned over toward Abby. "I told you that kid is dumb. D-U-M."

"I knew you'd be thrilled," Kiki was telling Justine, "when you saw the painting." Her huge hoop earrings glittered against her fat cheeks as she pointed toward the table.

Abby drew in her breath. On the table was the canvas that had been in the apartment. It was a picture of the hyacinth macaw. Abby nudged Potsie. "Hyacinth looks a little fat. But that picture is really good."

Then she caught Dan's eye. He grinned at her. It was a good thing he didn't know all the things she had thought about him this week.

She edged her way over to him. "Did you really dream about a gale?"

He looked down at her. "You'll never know."

"Come on. Tell me."

Dan grinned again. "Actually I dreamed of the police."

Abby raised her eyebrows. "Eggie told me that means good luck."

"First prize, thirty dollars," Justine yelled, "goes to Kiki Krumback. Even though she took my bird, you'll have to admit it's a wonderful likeness of my Lulu."

Everyone clapped.

"And a special prize," Justine yelled above the noise. "Twenty dollars for the most original artwork . . ."

"I bet I know . . ." Potsie began, and started to laugh.

". . . to Daniel Jones and Holly Monk for their"— Justine leaned over and read the sign that Dan had placed in front of the birdbath—"for their PURPLE PIGEON PURIFIER."

Everyone laughed. "It really was a good-luck dream," Abby said, thinking that Dan wouldn't need much of her reward money now.

At that moment, the door opened. In came Garcia and Witkowski.

"The mystery is solved," Justine shouted out to them. "The bird has returned."

"The mystery," Abby repeated. "Do you suppose we've solved Garcia's case?"

"The bird is worth two thousand dollars," Potsie said. "And it happened on Washington Avenue. It all fits."

They edged over to the detectives. "Guess who solved the mystery?" Abby asked Garcia.

Potsie turned to Witkowski. "And Abby and I get every cent of the reward."

Garcia smiled at them. "I guess you'll be too busy spending the money to work on another case."

Abby smiled back. "Never too busy." She pulled out her memo book and turned to a new page. "Anything exciting you need help on?"

FROM THE MEMO BOOK OF
DETECTIVE A. HYACINTH JONES

DATE: Half Thursday, April 8 and half Friday, April 9. (Too tired to do whole thing last nt.)

TIME: Couple of.

What to do with my half of reward mny.
1.   Save some (not too much).
2.   Buy cookbook for Eggie.
3.   Buy art stuff for Kiki Krumback. (If it weren't for Kiki, wd still be poor.)
4.   Buy shirts for Dan and Holly Monk. Put on front:
        WON WITH JUNK
5.   Buy pr. of binocs. for me. (Better than Dan's.)
6.   Pay man in token booth for subway ride.

About the Author
Patricia Reilly Giff is the author of *Fourth-Grade Celebrity, The Girl Who Knew It All,* and *Left-Handed Shortstop.* She lives in Elmont and Harvard, New York, with her husband and three children.

About the Illustrator
Anthony Kramer has illustrated a series of cookbooks and his work has appeared in *Cricket* magazine. He lives in New York City.